BEST

Best lesbian erotica of the

BEST
LESBIAN EROTICA
OF THE YEAR

VOLUME ONE

BEST
LESBIAN EROTICA
OF THE YEAR

VOLUME ONE

Edited by
D. L. KING

CLEiS
PRESS

Published in the United States by Cleis Press, an imprint of Start Midnight LLC, 101 Hudson Street, 37th Floor, Suite 3705, Jersey City, New Jersey 07302.

Printed in the United States.
Cover design: Scott Idleman/Blink
Cover photograph: iStock
Text design: Frank Wiedemann
First Edition.
10 9 8 7 6 5 4 3 2 1

Trade paper ISBN: 978-1-62778-216-6
E-book ISBN: 978-1-62778-217-3

"Mother Tongue," by Camille Duvall, was originally published in *Summer Love: Stories of Lesbian Holiday Romance*, edited by Harper Bliss and Caroline Manchoulas (Ladylit, 2015); "Act Two," by Tamsin Flowers, was originally published in *Al Fresco: Five Outdoorsy Tales of Lesbian Lust*, (Ladylit, 2015); "Crème Brûlée," by Sacchi Green, was originally published in *All You Can Eat: A Buffet of Lesbian Erotica and Romance*, edited by R. G. Emanuelle and Andi Marquette (Ylva, 2014); "Pledge Night," by Radclyffe, was originally published in *Girls on Campus*, edited by Sandy Lowe and Stacia Seaman (Bold Strokes, 2016).

CONTENTS

INTRODUCTION:
ACT ONE

I feel like I've finally arrived, being asked to edit *Best Lesbian Erotica of the Year*. And then, of course, I feel like an imposter; they got it wrong, they couldn't have meant me. The Best Lesbian Erotica series is so iconic and I feel so honored to join the great names in lesbian erotic fiction who have gone before me. This edition marks the twenty-first year of the book's continuous publication. That's a lot of history, and a lot of smut. I'm not going to talk about how this book legitimized the feelings of generations of women or how it helped pave the way to acceptance and normalcy (if there is such a thing—and if one would want to identify with a word like that). Those sentiments have echoed down the line of past series editors and they have said it so much better than anything I could hope to add. But I will tell you about what the experience was like for me.

After the reality set in, I settled back and began the work that would bring an anthology to life. I consider myself an old hand at editing erotica anthologies. I've done a good number of them and have the mechanics down. So I put out a call for submissions and waited until the deadline to begin reading—at least that was my plan. I knew, from friends who had edited *Best Lesbian Erotica,* that they got a large number of submissions, but I wasn't really prepared for the deluge that arrived in my inbox. I started reading a little early to get a handle on things and not fall hopelessly behind.

No problem, I thought, it'll be easy to weed out the poor and mediocre submissions. But there weren't all that many poor, or even mediocre stories. No, the writers did not make it easy for me. What that means is you, dear reader, hold a collection of truly excellent stories in your hand. At least I hope you will find them excellent. Tastes differ and what I find erotic may not always be what you find erotic. But this I can promise. Each of these gems is a superlative piece of storytelling—a world in microcosm and a piece of someone's soul. I know, that sounds a little highbrow for a work of erotica, and I don't mean it to. What I mean is that I stand in awe of these writers and am so happy they chose to share their stories with me so I could share them with you.

This book, like all my books, is eclectic. That's because my tastes are scattered. I'm like the child who can't stop picking flowers in a field because the next is even more beautiful than the last. There's no theme here, other than women and sex, but that's what you want in a book of lesbian erotica, isn't it? The stories meander from dramatic to funny to important to sad, from long-lost love to down and dirty raunch. I've often heard people say, "It's an anthology. Feel free to skip around." I always cringe when I hear that because (here's a little secret) I agonize over the order of the stories. I'm pretty sure all editors do. But I get down on the floor and move them around, like pieces on a game board. It takes a while, and I have to keep shooing the cat off them. But it's important for the order to work for me (and hopefully for you, if you don't skip around).

The first story—in this case, "Act Two," by Tamsin Flowers—

sets the stage for drama; it gets you primed and ready for all that will follow. And the last story, "A Sense of Coming Home," by P. A. Nox, brings you to where I hope you want to be—a new beginning. And, in between those two stories? The meandering path of life: a sorority initiation; a lover who knows your worth, even when you don't know it yourself; envy, jealousy and the heat of competition; meeting the kind of good, perfect girl you never thought you'd be into; karaoke night in your favorite girl bar. Like I said: life. Add the unexpected (because life does that from time to time), like a story of Victorian manners; a spy versus spy tale or that of an Apache and a curandera in 1800s Arizona; and then, just for fun, a revolutionary tale; of fetishistic clothing and the proletariat.

There are authors you've come to love and expect to find in a book of this caliber, like Sacchi Green, Radclyffe, Valerie Alexander and Annabeth Leong. There are old friends, like Tamsin Flowers and Roxy Katt. And then there are writers with whom you may not be familiar, but I'm betting you'll hope to see again and again, like Elna Holst, P. A. Nox, J. Belle Lamb and Samantha Luce.

Like I said: eclectic.

Yes, it's *Best Lesbian Erotica of the Year,* but it's also a D. L. King book. If you like that sort of thing, I think you'll be pleasantly surprised. If you don't know whether you like that sort of thing or not, I hope you'll also be pleasantly surprised. Enjoy the meandering. Sure, skip around if you must, but if you'd like to get into my headspace, read these snippets of life in the order laid out before you and be transported.

D. L. King
New York City

ACT TWO

Tamsin Flowers

I push the girl back roughly until she's pinned against the ancient stonemasonry. I've got one forearm across her chest. She can't move, but neither does she want to. We're deep in the shadows of a secluded archway, but even out in the open piazza, she willingly licked ice cream from my fingers, with a tongue that held the promise of other, sweeter explorations.

Her chest swells and falls under my arm and the cold, clammy air carries the dense smell of her sweat to my nostrils. I lean forward and catch her bottom lip between my teeth, sucking it into my mouth. Her body relaxes and she reaches one hand up to the back of my neck, pulling me closer so she can prolong the kiss.

I close my eyes. This is a moment I've imagined so many times. Not with this girl, particularly. But with similar faceless, nameless girls, who over the years, have fueled me in my single-minded determination to make the vision a reality. To put a face and a body to the fantasy. This girl, Mercy, has finally stepped into the role.

Why is she the one? What does she have in common with the girls I've conjured up in my mind?

They all share a lover. The lover Mercy has for real.

I push a knee up between Mercy's legs. She's wearing jeans and I press hard enough to feel the thickening of the fabric where the leg seams meet at the crotch. I rub against it, grinding it into her, and she moans without taking her mouth from mine.

Loud voices, speaking Italian, pass close to the arch and we freeze for a moment. Then I grab a handful of her short hair at the back and yank her head away from mine.

"Meet me tonight at nine in the Orto Botanico—the botanical gardens."

"I..." she stammers, then stops.

"Can you get away?"

"Earlier? Celestine dines at nine. She'll expect me to be there."

"I want you at nine."

I don't wait for her reply. I let go of her abruptly and leave the cool shadows for the bleached intensity of the piazza. My heart pounds as I walk away from her. Now, after so many years, I'll be able to repay Celestine Bouchard for what she did.

There was a time when Celestine and I were friends. When we first arrived to study opera at the Conservatoire in Paris. But not for long—it's hard to maintain a friendship with your biggest rival. And Celestine was a thief. First it was parts. She would audition for the parts I wanted, and she would petition directors for the parts I got. We were the two best singers in our year, so it was natural that we should be chasing the same dreams. But only one of us played dirty.

I've always had the more powerful voice of the two of us, but she scores on delicacy, refinement. Beauty. She makes the perfect princess. I'm better at playing the serving wench or the whore. The critics have said *Carmen* could have been written for me.

That didn't stop her taking the part, though, in our final year at the Conservatoire. But, my issues with Celestine aren't to do with the singing or which of us has the better voice.

Celestine Bouchard, feted by those who know absolutely nothing about opera as the greatest voice of a generation, stole the love of my life. It happened more than a decade ago, and I haven't not thought of my beautiful Suzanne for a single day since. Celestine took her out of spite, then broke her, like a spoiled child bored with a new toy within minutes. I couldn't pick up the pieces. No one could. I don't know where Suzanne is now, and I don't kid myself that if I found her we could have what we had before. So I've taken other lovers, plenty of them, while I've been waiting for the moment that Celestine should appear in the crosshairs of my sight. And now she has.

She's here in Trieste—it's the International Opera Festival— to play Cio-Cio San in *Madame Butterfly*. In a bitter twist of irony, I'm here to sing *Carmen*, the role we were tussling over when she stole Suzanne. If I can't take back what's mine, I can at least take what's hers. Mercy. The beautiful toy with which Celestine is currently amusing herself.

The city is enchanting and sultry as I wind through the narrow streets at dusk. An assignation after dark. Meeting my rival's lover in a silent garden. It's worthy of an opera plot. I'm on a mission to seduce and Mercy's sweet young flesh will taste all the sweeter with the knowledge that Celestine will be wondering where she is. There's a thrum of expectation pulsing through me, a delicious tension. The night air caresses the bare skin of my arms with a lover's touch and I hear cicadas singing in unseen courtyards and gardens as I walk by.

Tonight, Suzanne, I finally get to lay your ghost to rest.

I make my way on silent feet to the entrance of the Orto Botanico. Relief floods through me when I see that the gate's been left open a crack. My bribery didn't go to waste and now Mercy and I will have the moonlit gardens to ourselves. I slip inside, leaving the gate a little wider open than I found it. I'm several minutes early, so I don't imagine Mercy's here yet. In my experience, quarry runs late while predators have a tendency to arrive early. I walk slowly along the central path, past the empty ticket office, through a series of stone arches and up toward the lotus pond. This is where I want to make my play.

The air is heavily scented with honeysuckle and rosemary.

In my mind's eye, I see Suzanne, as she was when I saw her last. A lump forms in my throat but it makes me more determined to do what I'm about to do. Mercy will be mine and Celestine will taste the bitterness of regret.

A footfall behind me makes me start. I turn and look but there's no one there, no one on the path. Leaves rustle and I think…I think I hear a breath being drawn.

"Mercy?"

"No mercy."

Oh my god.

I recognize that voice. It's as familiar to me as my own.

"Celestine?"

Celestine Bouchard steps out of the shadows of a stone arch onto the moonlit path. It's been eleven years since I've seen her this close, in the flesh. I've pored over her picture in magazines, and I saw her sing once, from the very back of the Royal Opera House. But here she is, living and breathing, in front of me, in the dark and deserted Orto Botanico in Trieste. Long hair streaming down over her shoulders, almond-shaped eyes wide as she searches me out. In the creamy moonlight, she's as beautiful as she ever was. Because, of course, she's made enough money to hold on to her looks.

"Genevieve. Geneva." She's the only one who ever calls me Geneva. She looks me up and down inquisitively. "You've hardly changed."

"You're a little fatter, my love."

"It's good for my voice. You're looking a trifle bony."

"I weigh the same."

We reach impasse.

Mercy has spilled and my plan's thwarted. I turn on my heel. I'm not going to hang around and make small talk with the bitch.

"You took the bait. I knew you would."

What the hell?

I turn back to face her, looking at her askance. But I keep my mouth shut because I know she loves the sound of her own voice.

"See? You've just taken it again. You really are easy to manipulate, my sweet Geneva. I picked Mercy because she was so very like Suzanne."

I hadn't even seen it. No one was like Suzanne in my eyes. But taking a step back, looking at the girl through Celestine's eyes, I can see why she might think them alike. A certain physical resemblance, a similar economy of movement. The same dark eyes. Anger erupts deep inside me. Why should she want to bait me? It was she who did *me* wrong. I'm the injured party. I take a step toward her and she stands her ground, watching me with lazy eyes, a smile playing fleetingly on her lips.

Slapping Celestine as hard as I can gives me immense satisfaction. It's not quite the revenge I've imagined, but the sound of my palm making contact with her cheek cracks like a gunshot. She grunts softly but stays put. I'm begrudgingly impressed and I'm not sure what to do next. Damn the woman. I'm not going to engage with her further.

Again, I turn back toward the gate.

Her voice is quiet. I strain my ears to hear what she says.

"Have you ever wondered why I took Suzanne?"

No, I've never wondered that. Anyone would want Suzanne, even if they didn't already hate me. I carry on walking, quickening my pace to get away from her.

"Suzanne was never my type. Mercy isn't my type."

5

I don't want to stop. I don't need to hear more of whatever story she's weaving. But my feet slow their pace. At the next stone arch, I sink back into the shadows. Curiosity has got the better of me, and I know I'll regret it.

She slows too, sensing my presence without needing to see me, like a cat.

"Geneva? I know you're here."

As a singer, I can control my breathing. I make it shallow and silent.

Celestine pauses, listening. Then she speaks again.

"I never meant to hurt Suzanne. Just you. What happened with the girl was collateral damage, as they say. She was young and she got confused. She thought she was in love, but she meant nothing to me." Celestine leans back against the wall, standing not three feet from me. She knows exactly where I'm lurking. "It was so easy to tempt her away from you—not very bright, eager to believe the lies I told her."

Celestine's words bring Suzanne momentarily back to me. A faithful puppy with pale eyes and a gap-toothed smile. Then, not so faithful.

"I could never understand, cheri, why you took such undemanding lovers. Never a girl who could challenge your intellect. Never a woman who spoke her mind."

She pauses, I suppose to let me justify my choices. But I don't.

"Did you never want something more interesting to pass the time? Someone who could press the buttons in your mind, rather than just the one between your legs?"

I break cover. These are awkward questions that have come to me in sleepless hours. I walk fast, taking a sharp turn from the main path, up toward the glasshouses. I don't hear Celestine pursuing me, but I'm sure she hasn't finished with me yet. The woman's like a terrier—harrying till she gets her way, gets what she wants. My vocal parts. My lover. For her, it's as natural as breathing. What's the bitch after now, tonight, in the Botanical

Garden in Trieste? The satisfaction of seeing me break? Does she want to make me cry?

I won't fucking give it to her, whatever it is she wants.

The glasshouse door opens with a whine and I slip inside, enveloped by the heavy air. The fetid scent of decaying plant matter and overripe fruit assaults my nostrils and the damp heat makes my skin prickle. It's darker in here but the pale flagstones underfoot show the path ahead as I venture into the lush growth of the interior. I walk slowly to keep my footfalls silent. Large drops of water burst against my head, my arm, and when I brush past an overhanging branch, a flurry of droplets feels like rain.

I pray that she won't follow me, but conversely I'm not disappointed when I hear the door open and close behind me. Celestine and I have been playing these cat-and-mouse games for years. Of course, she isn't going to let things lie. Her cruelty has always fascinated me—the way she's able to take from others with no compunction, the way in which she feeds off the inner lives of fellow performers, giving nothing of herself in return. After leaving the conservatoire I avoided her for so long. I had to, to preserve myself and my self worth. Now, I can feel myself being drawn back toward her, mothlike to her aureole, unable to resist the bright flare of her presence.

I listen but there's nothing. I reach the pond at the center of the glasshouse and stop by the low stone wall that forms its edge. The huge lily pads are dappled with moonlight and I can just see the dark umber forms of the Japanese carp as they glide silently through the water. I watch two that seem set on a collision path, veering just enough to slide easily past each other on their way to opposite sides of the pool. Will I veer away from Celestine at this moment or will we collide? A collision has been a long time coming.

She appears on the other side of the pond and we stand, staring at each other.

"I don't believe that you never wonder why I took Suzanne."

I stare at her for longer. In the half-light she looks exactly as she did all those years ago. It's like seeing a ghost. My own past, confronting me. It's not comfortable.

"Because you hated me."

"No, I never hated you," she replies quickly. "My god, Genevieve, you thought I hated you? Never that."

"Your behavior toward me was hardly benign."

"I wanted you to notice me."

"To notice you? You loomed large in everything I did. I was obsessed with you."

Celestine's face clouds with anger.

"With my voice."

"You were my rival from the very first day. You snatched every part I ever wanted."

"For the same reason."

"To get my attention? You had it, Celestine."

"My voice had it. But you never saw me, the person to whom the voice was attached."

"We were both ambitious."

"We could have stayed friends."

My bark of laughter echoes against the glass.

"You and I? Never. In fact, Celestine, have you ever had a real friend?"

She ploughs through the pond with no thought of the fish or the lily pads. Water floods over the low wall and splashes my feet. I brace myself—it's her turn to slap me and her arm is already raised as she bears down on me. But as she steps up out of the water, her hand doesn't make contact with my face as I expect it to. It snakes around the back of my neck and grabs a handful of my hair. Celestine is six inches shorter than me, but standing on the rim of the pond, her eyes are level with mine. They burn with fury and with passion, and I can't tear myself away from her gaze.

"I want you."

It's as simple as that. I don't even know if it comes from my mouth or hers. I don't know who initiates the kiss—it doesn't matter. All I'm aware of is her tongue inside my mouth. My tongue inside her mouth. Wrapping together in a frantic, long-awaited duet. Blood roars in my ears and I feel light-headed. I stagger but she holds me firm. I hope she'll never release me, that our first kiss will last forever.

"Damn you! This is what it was all about," she says.

Her lips move against my teeth and the kiss endures. She's right. There's a decade of hate, love, obsession and regret bound up—and now finding release—in our connection.

I've never kissed Celestine before but her mouth is like a homecoming, a place I might have known in some other previous or parallel existence. I'm not given to believing in past lives or alternate universes, but there's something different about this kiss. Something particular that's been missing from other kisses. I can't even remember Mercy's mouth to compare it. And I've long since forgotten Suzanne's.

For god's sake stop analyzing.

I let myself go. My conscious mind slips away, bowing to the needs of my body. I become aware of the heat of Celestine's flesh, pressing against mine through summer linen. I run my hands up and down her back, feeling the rough weave under my fingertips. But I want to feel her skin and yielding flesh.

I break the kiss and step back. She drops down from the wall.

"Take off your clothes," I say.

"And you."

We strip and the moonlight makes our skin pale. We stare at each other's bodies. There's no rush now. We've established where we're headed, we both know what's going to happen. And we both know this is a three-act story. The overture is long forgotten. Act One was played out a decade ago. Now we pause, as Act Two nears its climax.

Celestine sighs. "You're identical to the you in my imagination."

"You're better," I say.

Our bodies collide. I grasp her by the shoulders and drop my mouth to the peak of one of her heavy breasts. Her breath whispers softly as the areola tightens. How did I not know I wanted this? Her?

"Come with me," she says, her torso twisting, pulling her nipple from my mouth.

I look up to her face as I straighten up, but she's turned away. She leads me by the hand along a raised path, climbing until we've reached a higher level of the glasshouse.

"Here," she says.

On either side of the walkway, velvet beds of dark moss look like black upholstery in the watery light. I push her and she falls willingly onto the puffy surface. I drop to my knees beside her. The moss is cool and damp against my skin and I want to feel it along the length of my body. I lie down next to her, rolling onto my side to face her, aware of a faint scratching and prickling underneath me.

Celestine cups one of her breasts in her hand, offering it to me, so I suck it back into my mouth. I can't process the words she murmurs in my ear. Sweet words, nothing words. My world is centered on the feel of her skin beneath my fingers and the taste of it in my mouth. Her flesh is soft and smooth. I let my hand sweep down the curve from her rib cage to her tiny waist and back out with the flare of her hips. She responds with a soft moan, her body pushing itself against my hand. Freeing her nipple from my mouth, I roll her onto her back and straddle her. I gaze down into her face but my own shadow makes it difficult to read her expression.

"Is this how it was meant to go? What you wanted?" I say.

"Yes."

She rears up and catches my lower lip between her teeth, biting down on it. Pain flares and that's fine with me. Our breasts brush against one another and she digs firm fingers into my hips.

I wrap my arms around her back and grind my hips into hers. She places a palm flat against my clit, her fingers lightly pressing their way between my lips. I spread my thighs wider to make it easier for her to fuck me with her hand. I'm ready for this now. I want it badly. Small thrills are sparking up and down my core, the muscles of my cunt searching for something to clench around.

She pushes two fingers up inside me, and I let go of her so I can lean back supported by my arms. This opens me up to her completely and she starts to fuck me hard, ramming into me and pulling out, sweeping her thumb across my clit momentarily, then slapping my cunt before shoving back into me harder than before. I gasp and arch my back.

The moonlight paints a checkerboard grid on my torso and turns Celestine's skin to pewter. She uses her free hand to hold me steady and underneath me, I can feel her hips flexing and pushing up. She planes my clit mercilessly with the ball of her thumb, circling it and rubbing it until my movements become frenzied and my breath ragged.

A climax bubbles up inside me, then bursts, washing through me, hot and cold, sharp and soft, so sweet, intensifying as Celestine keeps doing what she's doing. Sweat breaks out on my skin and my heart thunders in my chest. I collapse onto one side and she wraps me in an embrace, still fucking me, curling her fingers inside to find my G-spot and drawing out my pleasure until I have to push her away.

Act Two is over. The curtain falls. And in the interval, as I catch my breath for a moment, I must decide whether this will be a love story or a tragedy.

FUCKIN' NICE

Deb Jannerson

It all happened because some has-been rapper decided that Tyler Lite and I hate each other.

Apparently, I was in a blood feud with America's Most Oscar-Hopeful Sweetheart. I didn't even know about the lines until the press started calling:

> *When I find you in the corner, won't be fuckin' nice*
> *Bitch each other out like Tyler Lite and April Vice.*

God only knows where he gets this stuff. I've got to wonder if he just makes a collage out of words in teen magazines, like a chain-letter master. I'd never even met Tyler. As for the obnoxious yet somehow popular hip-hopper, he and I had spoken exactly once before. He had tried to pick me up, and failed. I had to wonder if this was supposed to be revenge.

My manager said I should have been thankful. Finally, a rumor about me that didn't involve girls in my bed! Oh, joy!

I found it both hilarious and sad that the sapphic speculation about me made him so nervous. He wouldn't let me actually say so, not yet, but I did have girls in my bed, and playing coy about it was starting to get silly. What year was this, 1950? At least he didn't make me outright lie. After all, sexual ambiguity was good for my tough chick, tomboy-by-Hollywood-standards image.

All of which made it even weirder that Mr. Middle-Aged Badass was putting us together in his shitty song. If you're going to make up a feud, shouldn't you do it between people of similar reputation? Tyler Lite was anything but a tomboy, despite the androgynous first name. She was sweet, quiet, safe. She had the look of a thousand other white women who are popular actors. Perfectly pleasant and bland. Even the tabloids couldn't seem to spin any scandalous stories about Tyler, or maybe they just couldn't be bothered.

Okay, I wasn't exactly a fan, but it's not like I had anything against Tyler. Nothing that would make me likely to "bitch her out" or whatever. That sexist pig.

Of course, now Tyler and I would have to meet. At least, we'd have to "meet," as in, smile and say hi and act nice for a minute with cameras around. If either of us let concern cross our faces, the press would catch it and make this bullshit even bigger. We had to be perfect, unflappable young stars, the pop-rocker and the actor ingénue, just tickled that this silly old guy thought we didn't get along.

"April! Over here!"

I hooked my thumbs into my ironic suspenders and gave a small, untroubled smile at the ring of cameras as I stepped out of the limo. I had no idea which of the paparazzo was screaming at me and, ultimately, it didn't matter. I was to give them all the fake, 50 percent smile, the one that didn't crease my face in any way supposedly unseemly to the media. I sure hoped they appreciated it, because that teeth-bleaching treatment the week before had been agony. I tried to ignore what the camera folk were yelling, but I've never been good at that.

"April! Is it true you're dating Jack McGruff?" *What? Gross.*

"Ms. Vice! Is your song, 'Torn Apart,' about a girl?" *The word is "woman," thanks.*

"April Vice, are you gonna fight with Tyler?" *Theeeeere it is.*

I glanced around, nonchalant, until my eyes landed on Tyler Lite. With perfect posture, she stood in a gauzy lavender dress, silver heels, and that slightly curled hair that no one has naturally. She was smiling at me demurely, pretending to make conversation with another starlet but no doubt waiting for our big media moment. I'm sure her manager had prepped her well. Tonight's awards show was only for musicians, and she's more into acting these days, so I might even have been the reason she was there.

Showtime. "Tyler!" I squealed, stepping toward her slowly. I noticed flashbulbs pointed at my boots and groaned inwardly. I already knew I'd be accused of dressing "inappropriately" in the press, even though my footwear was probably just as expensive as everyone else's. "It's so nice to meet you, finally!"

She held out her hand like a princess. "It sure is! I'm a big fan." We shook limply and grinned at each other—not at the cameras, never at the cameras. Mission accomplished. Now I could focus on the important stuff, like how good my odds were for Best New Artist.

I snuck into the posh bathroom just before showtime. I was supposedly touching up my dark makeup, but actually I just needed a break from all the hangers-on and attitude. You've never seen such a fancy lavatory, I promise. Apart from the section of the room taken by stalls, the walls were covered in those super-Hollywood mirrors with the circular lights all around them. An enormous wraparound couch spanned the perimeter beneath them, like a big version of those seats in picture windows. I stared into one of the lit-up mirrors, feeling like Marlene Dietrich.

"Good work out there." I started, and in the mirror, my eyes met Tyler Lite's. She had just stepped in and was smirking at my reflection from inside the door.

"Yeah." I chuckled and rolled my eyes. She had flustered me, bursting in when I probably looked like I was checking myself out, but I played it cool. "I think we put that feud rumor to rest."

"All in a day's work." Tyler's eyes went to the ground, giving me a good view of her super-shiny eye shadow. "I wasn't kidding, though. About being a fan. I love your music. It's so... empowering."

"Oh." I knew she was probably just being polite, but I felt awkward. "Thanks. You were great in *Ambivalent Sunrise*." I totally hadn't seen it. Who's the actor now? Everyone said Tyler had done well, and I didn't doubt it, but flicks about straight people being sad are not my thing.

Tyler's face turned pink. She actually blushed. It was so precious that I should have wanted to puke, but...she just seemed so earnest. Most performers look less perfect in person, but that wasn't quite true for Tyler. She looked more real but, somehow, just as flawless and alluring.

I couldn't help it; I was charmed. Her shyness reminded me of someone I had gone to high school with before dropping out to do music full-time. Not to put too fine a point on it, let's just say she was a cheerleader and it didn't end well for me. If you've listened to my album, you can probably figure out the rest.

"Can I ask you something?" Tyler breathed, still not meeting my eyes.

I started to get nervous. "My boobs aren't fake," I joked. Not my strongest moment, but whatever.

Tyler's eyes came back to me. Actually, they went right to my chest, and then darted away again. I felt a tingling in my fingertips. Suddenly, I had some idea of where this was going. "Is it true?" Tyler whispered, stepping toward me. "That you're... That you like—"

"Women?" I stepped closer and, with some difficulty, made eye contact. Tyler looked scared but determined.

"Yeah."

I put my hands in my pockets and shrugged, taking another step. "Some of them. Why?" I smiled coquettishly. "Got someone in mind?"

Tyler surprised me by making the first move. She put an arm around my shoulder and kissed me hard. I backed her up against the wall and opened my mouth to her, playing with her just-brushed, minty tongue. She made a soft, yearning sound against my lips, and I felt it like a lightning bolt to the cunt.

"Fuck," I moaned as our mouths got wetter. Tyler wrapped both arms around me tight, pulling my body flush against hers. I could feel her nipples through her dress. Who knew America's Sweetheart goes braless? She licked my neck from collarbone to ear, and I shivered.

When she tried to put a leg around me, though, it snapped back down almost immediately. Tyler's cute little dress had not been made for situations like this. Well, the good thing about clothes is that they come off. I pulled my head back and nodded toward the nearest, and roomiest, stall, raising an eyebrow.

"What are we, at prom?" She rolled her eyes, looking, just for a minute, like the prissy cliché I had imagined. "Let's get out of here."

That, I didn't expect. "You'd leave the show? It's only just starting. What about the photo ops?"

"Screw it." Tyler shrugged. Her attitude was a nice surprise; then again, she wasn't the one up for awards. But I could hardly say that without sounding like an epic tool, not to mention a hypocrite.

"Wait." I fished my felt-tip eyeliner out of my bag and yanked a paper towel out of the dispenser. Leaning the sheet against the wall, I scrawled OUT OF ORDER. I wouldn't be able to use the eyeliner again, but talk about small sacrifices. I pulled open the bathroom door, makeshift sign in hand, then realized I had no way to stick it to the outside.

"I got you." Snapping open her ridiculous clutch, Tyler pulled out an intensely sparkly pink vial. She unscrewed the top, which turned out to be a sponge tip to a lip gloss, marked the back of my towel in a neat line, and patted it onto the door almost daintily.

I waited for it to fall down, but apparently her lip goo was sticky enough to make this work. "I'm impressed," I admitted, swinging the door closed again to seal us inside. "But you're not wearing that, are you?" I ran a finger over my mouth, which was thankfully adhesive-free.

"Nah." She smacked her own lips at me and grinned. "This is a long-wear lipstick night."

I lunged toward her again.

We tumbled down onto the wraparound couch, which was even softer than it had looked. Tyler sank into the red velvet, looking right at home as I straddled her and undid her zipper. She wriggled her top half out of the dress, revealing perfect, medium-sized breasts with the most erect nipples I had seen this side of winter. I ran my face down her smooth skin, working my mouth over one of Tyler's nipples while I played with the other with my fingers. I used my lips and tongue while my hand circled and lightly pinched.

"April," she sighed, tugging at my suspenders and tight black jeans. Her hands danced around and found my fly. As she pushed me onto my back on the velvet, Tyler leaned into my ear. Her breath tickled as she huskily whispered, "I've been fucking myself to your picture for months."

I groaned and let her tear off my jeans. At this point, I was afraid they would look like I'd spilled a drink on them if they stayed on; I was so hot for Tyler. Besides, all I wanted was her skin on mine. Well, that and… "Show me."

Tyler stopped short. "What?"

"Show me how you fuck yourself, you naughty lady."

Tyler's eyes widened. She jumped up for long enough to scoot down the rest of her dress, then lay back down spread-eagled. I could only stare. Tyler Lite now wore nothing except a pair of heels and a flimsy white thong covered in tiny, colorful jewels. Her panties had a G-string, so there was only a tiny line of cloth between me and her pussy, and I could see the edges of her labia peeking out of either side. Wetness soaked the middle of the string and spread out shiny over Tyler's inner thighs. I have no idea how long I just looked, hypnotized, before Tyler cooed, "Like what you see?"

"Fuck," I moaned again, feeling like I might explode. As I began yanking off the rest of my clothes, Tyler brought both hands down between her legs and started to play around. She slid one hand inside her thong, all five fingers working over her clit. With the other hand, she ran a finger down the soaked line of her underwear, right over her pussy, then dipped inside. Within half a second, her finger was all the way inside her. She pulled it halfway out, its bottom half glistening, then quickly glided it back in.

"Care to share?"

"Mmm." Tyler pulled the finger back out and stuck it deep into my mouth. I sucked hard; she tasted sweet. With my tongue and teeth, I pulled every bit of fluid off Tyler's hand, and then climbed on top of her.

I lay astride Tyler's thigh and kissed her again, pressing my own thigh between her legs. We both gasped at the contact. I rubbed back and forth a little, feeling my clit go white-hot at the friction. Tyler rocked beneath me, mouth open in pleasure as I sucked her bottom lip. Within seconds, both our thighs were slick where we connected.

Tyler traced her tongue along the insides of my lips as she started rocking against me faster. I could feel her clit, hard as a marble, rubbing my thigh as she made little noises into my mouth. It felt so warm that I wondered, for a split second, if it would leave a mark. I wouldn't have minded.

"Fuck me, April," she hissed fiercely. "Fuck me."

I rode her thigh faster and harder, starting to feel light-headed. I cupped Tyler's breast and grunted as we went back and forth again and again, each time feeling more excruciatingly wonderful. My crotch tingled so hard that I felt like every cell was electrified, and I pressed my face into Tyler's neck, eager for what I knew would happen next.

My climax ripped through me, making me shake hard against Tyler's body as I gasped. I soaked her leg with my glossy heat, mouth open against her skin. Tyler breathed faster as I came, and partway through she cried, "April! Fuck!" and began vibrating herself. She nearly sobbed as her body thrust against mine. I could feel her labia clenching and releasing against the skin of my thigh, and I swear it was the most erotic sensation I've ever felt.

As we lay there, cooling down, I heard the opening number of the show wrap up. "Shouldn't we get you back out there?" Tyler panted, nudging my arm. "You might have to give an acceptance speech."

I chuckled. "I guess."

We got up, not in any particular hurry, and began putting our clothes back on. Tyler stepped back into her lavender dress and pulled it up. A jagged sound went through the air. "Oh!" Tyler found a mirror—not hard, given where we were—and examined the tear that had just formed down the side of her dress, next to the bust. "Well…shit."

"No worries." I tossed her my jacket. It was shrunken and leather with a diagonal zipper; hardly her style, but it was all we had. "Just do this up. You can keep it, even. No one will notice a thing."

"Yeah, right!" Tyler rolled her eyes again but couldn't suppress a smile. "Won't you be cold?"

"I'm a badass. We don't get cold." I almost managed to say it with a straight face. Almost, but not quite.

Tyler shook her head and reapplied her lipstick before we went back to the show.

By the following morning, I didn't quite feel as blasé about our encounter. The press would be trying to dig up dirt like never before, now that I was an award-winning artist and shit. And, as we all know, when they can't dig up dirt, they create it. I took my time making coffee, gathering my nerve to open my laptop.

As a rule, I try to avoid those gossip sites. The first few times, it was pretty cool to see myself, but the stories were always so bogus that they made me angry. That day, I had to know: Had the sapphic speculation reached a fever pitch? Who had noticed our midnight outfit swap?

I steeled myself and clicked onto the most notorious site of all. My heart jumped into my throat at the first picture: Tyler in her dress and my jacket, loitering on the red carpet after the show.

Then I saw the caption: *IS TYLER LITE GOING PUNK?*

All I could do was laugh.

THE LAST TIME

Annabeth Leong

I should tell *her* this is the last time. I've never done that, but I could.

Every time she texts me, Thea says we won't see each other again after this one final fuck, but then she also claims, to anyone who asks, that she's straight. She has her reasons, but that doesn't make this any easier.

I can't trust myself either. Her text comes through after ten, but my phone is turned up loud and the ping gets me out of bed. I'd be lying if I said I wasn't waiting for it. Even while I think about how I'm not going to put up with this forever, I'm finding her favorite skirt and buttoning it on, stuffing my bag with lube and toys she likes, crumpling up my pride and shoving it into a corner of my mind well hidden by my lust and our history.

I can't follow the speed limit on the way to her place.

Thea used to be my actual girlfriend. In college, she sported a buzz cut to die for, rocked flannel shirts and steel-toed boots and took me to see Tegan and Sara for our first anniversary.

Outside Lupo's, downtown, after the show ended, we waited in an alley by the tour bus in the cold, hoping for a glimpse of the musicians. There was a whole crowd of us there, sweat from the press of people inside drying and freezing in our hair as we stood on our toes to see over each other and crammed our bodies into awkward spaces.

Thea helped me climb onto a narrow concrete wall that divided the alley from the parking lot beside it. From there, we had a great view of the tour bus and the side door of Lupo's, but the footing was precarious. She hooked an elbow around a lamppost for balance and held me around the waist with her other arm.

Our increased height exposed us to the cutting wind. I pressed closer to her, shivering in my short skirt and leggings, greedy for the warmth of her body. She folded one side of her oversized motorcycle jacket over my right shoulder and tightened her grip on me. I settled into the animal scent of leather, and of Thea.

There is a way that being in a crowd can make you feel private—almost secluded, though in fact you are the opposite. I drifted into that place as the minutes stretched into half an hour and beyond and my lower legs began to numb from holding the same position.

That trance was probably the reason I didn't stop her when the hand on my waist shifted and started crawling up my skirt. Instead, I remained perched on the wall, depending on her to help me stay in place, as her fingertips brushed first my outer thighs, then my inner thighs, and made their slow, determined way to my pussy.

She tapped my clit with her half-curled index finger, as if pointing it out to me. Each light impact sent a shiver through me. She paused, pressed more firmly and gave me a circular rub through my leggings and underwear. I gasped, and then immediately looked around to check whether anyone had noticed what she was doing to me. I felt Thea smile into my hair.

Shifting her mouth to my ear, she murmured, "We're going to be standing here for a while. But I want to fuck you *now*."

I whimpered and pressed my ass against her. Before I met her, I didn't believe people could need each other chemically, didn't understand doing foolish things for the sake of sexual gratification.

Hooking an arm back over her neck for balance, I spread my legs a few inches, too focused on her fingers and my clit to care how shaky that made my position on the wall.

"Do you like these leggings?" Thea asked. "Would you be upset if something happened to them?"

She tugged the stretchy fabric. I wanted her fingers back on my clit.

"Do whatever you want." I barely recognized my voice. It was so full of naked need. "I bought them to impress you, anyway."

"I'm impressed," Thea said, and used a corner of one short fingernail to open a hole along the seam, just over my pussy. "Now let's see if I can impress you, too." She gripped the edge of the ripped fabric and tore. Cold air hit my inner thighs, and I cringed at what seemed like a loud, obvious noise. My thin, silky thong felt like it wasn't covering me at all.

A second later, Thea made sure it wasn't, yanking the fabric to one side and plunging a finger into me.

I clenched my jaw to keep from moaning.

"You know," Thea whispered into my ear, "I've only ever felt your pussy wet. I never have to get you ready. Your body is always begging for me to fuck you."

It was true, but I didn't want to admit it. "Don't be cocky," I muttered.

"Why shouldn't I be? You're about to come all over my hand, and then after that you'll let me do anything I want to you."

I opened my mouth to protest, but my cunt had already begun to ripple around her fingers. I twisted my head to one side as I struggled not to cry out, and when I did, I caught a glimpse of someone watching us, smirking.

In any other situation, I would have cared. I would have stopped. Thea was still touching me, though, tearing the hole in my leggings even wider so she could get more of her hand into my pussy.

I don't remember if we saw any more of Tegan and Sara that night. What I do remember is coming for Thea, over and over, indifferent to the cold, to who might have seen us, to anything other than her body and my need for it.

I had no idea it would be our last time together as girlfriends.

I park in front of her building, in my usual spot, and wonder if any of her neighbors recognize my car. I wish I had put on clothes that were more obviously gay, wish I had revved the engine louder on my way into the lot. She wouldn't be happy if anyone noticed me, but I can't help wanting to leave a mark that can't be erased.

The night is too warm to be comfortable. I sniff as I pass under a stand of trees. Because it's late, my allergy medicine is wearing off. The light in Thea's window is on.

My body knew her at once, but my brain didn't. I stood in the grocery store line trying to understand why I was so instantly aroused by someone who wasn't my type.

I have mostly dated butches. I like muscular arms, the way boxer shorts look on a woman, and a whole lot of swagger.

The woman who had captured my attention had on a calf-length dress in a shapeless, conservative cut, wore her hair long and unstyled, and carried a tote bag emblazoned with the logo of a fundamentalist church. Not my type for a lot of reasons.

Her shoes were the gayest thing about her, but I knew I shouldn't read too much into sensible flats.

Her arms, though... She had forearm definition, and her

three-quarter sleeves seemed suspiciously tight. I couldn't prevent myself from drifting into a fantasy of this woman above me using all that muscle to drive into me the way that really counts.

She got to the front of the line and turned back to pull groceries out of her cart. Impossibly, I recognized Thea.

That woman *had* been above me. I had felt the force of those strong arms, and I had loved every moment of it. My inner thighs quivered as my body relived the experience right there beside the tabloids, breath mints and deeply discounted beef jerky.

I couldn't prevent myself from blurting out her name. She flinched at the sound of my voice.

I had barely seen her since the night of the concert, and not at all since college. She had gone over to her parents' place without me the evening after Tegan and Sara, and the next time we met up, she avoided my eyes and made flimsy excuses. I never really found out why we went from wild passion on the street to nodding awkwardly at each other in the hallways.

Thea apparently did not want to give me a chance to ask any questions. After the cashier finished ringing her up, she pushed her cart out to the parking lot faster than a shopping-spree winner on a game show.

I dropped my basket of groceries at my feet and ran after her, ignoring people's curses and startled exclamations as I pushed past them.

She had bags to load into her trunk, and even with her strong arms, she couldn't do that before I caught up with her. I grabbed her car's bumper, panting, grateful for every minute of cardio I'd put in recently at the gym.

"Thea, wait."

"We shouldn't be talking, Mel."

"Why not?"

She gave me a significant look, but I refused to interpret it for her. Besides, the main thing I got from it was a fresh jolt of attraction when she met my eyes intensely. I could tell she felt it, too. She'd always had a way of tossing her head like an animal about to charge just before she kissed me, and she did it now, her strange new long hair floating around her face as she did.

"Why not?" I repeated.

She cleared her throat and dropped her eyes. "My parents will hear about it if I backslide."

"If you backslide? I just wanted to talk to you, find out how you've been."

"I've been well." Her voice was reedy, less confident than I'd ever heard it. She moved as if to square her shoulders, but she wasn't actually standing tall.

"For Christ's sake, Thea." She frowned, and I wondered if it was because I'd taken the Lord's name in vain. "For...Pete's sake, I guess. No, forget that. I have no idea who Pete is. How about for *your* sake? What happened to you?"

Was that a smile that flashed across her lips? If it was, it faded quickly. "I can't talk about it."

"Thea, we used to be in love. I still care about you. You can tell me, whatever it is."

She flinched again, and I wished she would stop doing that. She glanced over each shoulder, and then turned back to me. "Lower your voice, Mel. Most people don't know about my past."

"*Our* past."

Thea bit her lip. "I'm straight," she said, her voice wavering. "I'm sorry if that disappoints you."

That hurt my pride. "Why would I be disappointed? Maybe I've got a superhot new girlfriend who makes me come way harder than you ever did. Maybe I think back on what you and I had, and it all seems childish to me." I had to stop talking, because I found myself suddenly on the verge of tears.

Thea's mouth twitched into a shadow of her old cocky smile. My face heated as my body reacted to it the way it always had. "None of that is true and you know it," Thea said.

That was the woman I'd never been able to forget. I wanted to climb into the backseat of her sedan right then and there.

I grabbed for Thea's hand, but she snatched her fingers away. "I can't, Mel. Don't you understand that I can't?"

She ran for the driver's-side door, but I didn't chase her. I just folded my arms across my chest. "No," I called after her. "Because I know you can."

Tonight, I've got half a mind to slap her hands away when she tries to touch me, lift up my skirt, show her my lacy black thong and tell her she can only have my pussy if she cops to what she sees in our future. Does she think she can play straight forever?

I push the buzzer beside the main door of the building. My pulse races as I wait for the sound of the lock releasing for me. The elevator is too slow for my taste. I dart around the corner and yank open the door to the stairwell.

I hustle up four flights, but pause at the top. I'm always a little worried that I'll get this close but she'll decide not to let me in.

This time, though, the door is cracked for me. I swear I can already smell the rose and lime scent of her body lotion, even from out in the dingy hallway.

My strides get longer. I slip through the space she opened for me, and I don't want to be furtive about it, but I am. Her entranceway and living area are dark. The only light in the apartment is coming from the bedroom, and that seems like such an appropriate metaphor for our relationship that it makes me a little sick. I head toward it. That's all I've ever been able to do.

Thea's first late-night text came two days after I ran into her at the grocery store. I had the same number I'd used in college, but she'd apparently changed hers.

She said she wanted to talk, and I was stupid enough to believe her.

I drove to meet her at IHOP, but before I could walk into the restaurant, a car in a secluded corner of the parking lot flashed its lights. Its passenger door popped open. I walked over and got inside, and Thea kissed me before I could say a word.

She was half starved, pawing at me with a shocking lack of coordination. I needed her just as badly, so I climbed over the gearshift, awkwardly inserted myself between the steering wheel and her body, and let her get away with touching me without explaining anything.

I choked on the humidity of her closed-in car and strained to see her face in the dim light from the restaurant's sign. She kissed me as if the inside of my mouth contained water, air, light and food, but her hands stayed outside of my clothes, and soon my body was hot and wet while my mind roiled with confusion.

She tore a button off my shirt, and then froze and began to apologize.

"Stop it," I said, and tore another button off myself.

I grabbed her hand. Looking into her eyes as best I could in the darkness, I guided her fingers into the space made by the missing buttons, leading her to the edge of my bra. Thea gasped, and her fingers fluttered. I helped her even more, tugging my underwire upward to let my breasts spill out beneath. One of them landed in her hand.

"Christ," Thea said, and I grinned, because I hoped that meant she hadn't disappeared entirely into that fundamentalist church. I opened the rest of the shirt, and she pressed her face to my chest.

Thea sucked my nipples, and I arched into it. She made a sound that was far too close to a sob, and I swallowed hard. Sympathetic tears started in my own eyes, unbidden.

To stop the emotion from overwhelming me, I focused on the physical. I found Thea's other hand and pulled it under my skirt, trapped it between my thighs, let her feel how wet I'd gotten while we kissed.

"Fuck me." I wanted to command her, but instead the words came out in the begging tone I'd used when we were together.

"I shouldn't," Thea moaned. Her fingers were already creeping under the elastic of my panties. I tilted my hips to give her better access.

"I think you should," I told her. I wanted to go on, to scold her for pretending to be someone she wasn't, but my words broke off in a gasp. The new Thea might have been tentative and guilt stricken, but she still had no trouble finding my G-spot. "Yes…"

I grabbed fistfuls of her hair for balance. I wanted to touch her, too, to drive her wild the same way she was doing to me, but the rhythm she set didn't give me room to do anything but lean my forehead on the top edge of the driver's seat and whimper. I'd masturbated since we were last together, hundreds of times, and I'd fucked and been fucked by other women, some of whom were good in bed. No one was like Thea. It felt like my body had been asleep since we were lovers, as if only Thea had the key that could unlock my truest, deepest orgasm.

I was well on my way to coming, but she pulled her hand away at the last second.

"No! Wait! I'm so close."

"I know." Thea lifted me off her lap, her arms as strong as ever. With only a little help from me, she propelled me back to the passenger side of the car, and then slipped down into the space between my legs.

Her tongue felt so good it hurt. I wanted to watch her, but the sensations were too intense. I squeezed my eyes shut, a few tears leaking out the corners. She had to hold me by the hips to keep me from squirming away.

I'd gotten too close and then stopped, and I couldn't work up to coming again. My clit was trapped just on the edge of climax. The slightest heat of her breath made me jerk and tremble and tense, but nothing could take me over the edge.

She moaned softly as she played with me. I grabbed the head-rest behind me and dug my fingers in for all I was worth. The moment was excruciating, but I never wanted it to end.

Soon, I found myself trying to hold back my orgasm, just because I wanted to keep her between my legs. Thea was much too clever for that, though. She slid fingers into me as she licked and then, ever so gently, began to toy with the entrance to my ass. No one but Thea had ever touched me there. A flood of memories rushed through me—of first times, of hot times, of intense times.

Then they all faded behind the force of *this* time. As the very tip of her index finger slipped into my ass, she captured my clit between her lips, sucking gently and tapping it with her tongue.

I sobbed as I came, clawing at her hair. I said foolish, stupid things in the moments afterward, about how I'd never stopped loving her, about how I needed her body always, about how I was glad we were back together.

She came up to join me in the seat, but she wouldn't let me touch her in return, and she wiped her chin harshly with a tissue from the glove compartment.

"Thea, what's the matter?"

"I have to go home."

"Now?"

She pulled my head to her chest, stroking my hair with a touch too light for my taste. She took a deep breath. "You never met my parents," she said.

I made a small sound of acknowledgment.

"The night after the concert, when I went to see them, they wanted to pull me out of school. They said college was corrupting me. Someone saw me with you, in that alley out back of Lupo's."

"They can't have been up to anything super-pious them-selves, if they—"

"That doesn't matter. I was never a good liar. I couldn't deny the story. I couldn't..." She stopped talking, her grip tightening on me. "I couldn't deny how I felt about you, what you were to me."

"Why didn't you tell me? I would have helped you. I would have done anything."

"Shh. I know. If it had been just about me, I would have told them to fuck off. But it wasn't. My sister was a senior in high school, and they weren't going to let her go to college at all."

"Assholes."

"I would have found a way to make it work, gone into debt, whatever. My sister didn't sign up for that, though. I couldn't put her through that just because of my selfish desires."

"You're not selfish."

She tilted my chin up and kissed me like she owned me. "Babe. You know I am."

I didn't agree, but I didn't argue.

"I asked them what they wanted me to do, and I'm—" She gestured at her long hair. "I'm doing it. All of it. I should have told you the truth. You deserved better. You still do." She tucked hair away from my forehead. "What the hell are you doing here? Hiding with me in a parking lot outside of IHOP?"

"Thea—"

She shook her head, cutting off whatever I'd been about to say. I could have persuaded her that night. I could feel the power I had over her. I thought of Thea's sister. Did I have the right to demand that Thea make a gesture that affected someone else, too?

"We can't do this again," she said. "This has to be the last time."

"Neither one of us is selfish," I said bitterly. I ran back to my car before I lost my dignity and begged.

Thea isn't in the bedroom. I see it empty, mutter to myself and then hear something behind me.

I turn back to see her shape on the couch, mostly hidden by the darkness. "Thea? Are you okay?"

"No," she answers.

I go to her, kneeling on the cushion beside her, touching her face and finding it wet. Then I freeze, because the long hair is gone. I realize that I can smell her old leather scent for the first time in forever, but there's also something dusty that tickles my nose. My heart starts to beat even faster than it did on the way over for what I thought would be another intense but secretive lay.

"What's going on?" I ask.

"My sister came out. She basically gave my parents the finger. Says she'll deal with college on her own, and they can go ahead and disown her if they want."

"That's badass," I say. "That's good, right?"

Thea pulls me into her lap, kissing me, crying on me, clutching at me. "I guess," she says between sobs. "When I heard, all I could think about was you. What I did to you... The time we could have had together." She takes my hand and puts it on her short hair. "I want to go back to how things were."

That makes me want to join her tears. I lean my forehead against hers and fumble for the light. "We can't," I say. "We can only be who we are now."

When I pull back, Thea's face is swollen from crying, but it's also bare and open. Her fingers are clutching my hips hard enough to bruise, but I don't mind. Hope is rising in my heart.

I ease her hands away from me and walk deliberately to the big picture window cut into the wall of her living room. Standing in front of it, illuminated by the lamp behind me, I undo my buttons, slide out of my skirt.

"Mel?" Thea says.

"I never cared who saw us fucking," I tell her, unclasping my bra, pushing my underwear down my legs. "Not at Lupo's. Not at IHOP. Not anywhere." I turn to face her. The way her eyes widen at the sight of me makes me feel beautiful and free. "Now neither of us has to care."

Instead of the last time, this feels like the first. She comes to me, and I come for her.

YOU HAVE THE RIGHT TO REMAIN NAKED

Samantha Luce

Son of a bitch, I grumble in my head. I'd missed my moment yet again. Jaz was already home. On her way to the shower, she'd removed the heavy gun belt. It hangs from the hook near the door. I reach to touch the slightly worn leather. It's still warm and just a tad moist. I can still hear the shower running. Nevertheless I steal a quick glance around the compact home to make sure she's nowhere in sight before I give completely in to temptation and bring my face close enough to rub the leather against my cheek. A soft moan escapes my lips.

Not long ago this leather strap had been wrapped around her waist. How many times had she grasped this belt during the day to hoist it higher on her hips? No matter how snug she cinched it, the damn thing was always sliding lower. Sure, I know it's the pull of gravity making it drop lower on her hips. It dips without the same lusty urgency that makes me slide down her sculpted body whenever we're together. Doesn't mean I don't envy that it gets to spend the day wrapped snugly around her.

There's a sweet spot just below where the belt normally rests on her hips. That apex between her thighs is my new safe place. It keeps me warm and blocks out all of life's insanity. I'd discovered this safe haven only three short months ago.

A fender bender in rush-hour traffic had brought us together. I was fuming. I had the right of way. I was on my way home after a long day. All I wanted was a glass of wine and some mindless reality TV to make me forget the mountains of paper threatening to bury me at the office. Instead I was stuck on the side of the road, my tire flat, the driver's side rear door sunken in about a foot, and a man in his eighties, who drove a tank disguised as a Buick, sitting across from me, looking sad and apologetic. The bumper of his car had only a minor dent. Luckily, we were both traveling solo and neither one of us was injured.

I saw the flashing blue light in my rearview mirror and was grateful and stressed at the same time. I knew I wasn't at fault, but cops always make me nervous. Any chance encounter I'd had with them normally ended with me getting a ticket or dragged back to school and told never to skip again.

The cop who dismounted the black-and-white motorcycle that day made me nervous for a whole new slew of reasons. She was tall, athletic and wore the tight black-and-white uniform the way Danica Patrick wears her racing suit, confidently and sexily. When she removed her helmet, her long blonde hair tied back in a ponytail fell loose and grazed the collar of her crisp white shirt. After determining neither one of us needed medical attention, she spoke to the older man first.

I tried not to stare at her as she spoke in hushed tones. I grabbed my cell phone and clicked on various apps just to have something else to look at. Every thirty seconds or so, my eyes were drawn back to the beautiful officer with the soft, throaty voice. I couldn't hear her when she was at the other driver's car, but that didn't stop me from watching her perfect Cupid's bow lips. They weren't painted. It actually didn't look like she had on any makeup at all. Perhaps a small amount of lip gloss or

ChapStick to help combat the moist Florida heat, but that was all. She didn't need anything else.

About twenty minutes later, another Buick pulled up beside the other driver's vehicle. An elderly female got out and rushed to the man's side. The flaxen-haired cop made her way over to me. "You sure you're okay, Emma?" she asked me. There was a small bead of sweat near her temple. It had gathered just enough moisture to slowly trickle down her cheek and jaw.

The trajectory of the moisture held me captivated. The urge to follow its salty trail with my tongue was overwhelming. My lips parted, tongue darting out, but I held back and licked my lips instead.

"Emma?" She'd removed her dark sunglasses. A look of concern caused her bright green eyes to narrow.

"I'm fine." I flashed her the smile I keep on reserve when I'm courting a new client for business. "Just daydreaming. Is Harry all right?"

"Yes, just a bit shaken. His wife just arrived. She'll drive him home. One of their sons is going to pick up his car later." She paused, pulled a few sheets from her pad and handed them to me. "He admitted he was at fault. I've collected all his information and issued him a citation for causing an accident. You'll just need to file the claim and his insurance will cover your repairs. The official accident report will be available at the precinct in three days if you need a copy. Do you have any questions?"

A few questions drifted through my mind. *Are you single? Do you like girls? What's your favorite position? Can I take you home and lick you until you come a hundred times on my tongue?*

I shook my head and smiled. I didn't think it'd be a good idea for me to verbalize a response. The vision in front of me was making me want to lose all my inhibitions. I figured it must have been a combination of the heat, her beauty and the damn uniform. The knee-high leather boots and shiny silver badge certainly didn't hurt either.

She gently kicked the flat tire with the toe of her boot, and then knelt down to get a closer look. "It's a shame about the tire. It doesn't look like the wheel well has been compromised. The axle looks fine too. Do you have a spare?"

Is it my imagination? I wondered. *Or is her gaze lingering just a second or two longer than necessary on my legs?* The stockings I wore suddenly felt tighter under her stare. "I do have a spare, but I've never changed a tire before," I answered. My eyes never wavered, but hers did. They flitted lower to watch my mouth as I spoke. She coupled the flirtatious glances with smiles that somehow balanced between shy, confident and sexy.

When she told me to cancel the tow truck because she would change the tire, it seemed only natural for me to thank her by offering to buy her dinner. She accepted, and the rest, as they say, is history, or in our case, *herstory*.

"Hey, babe," Jaz's voice brings me out of my reverie. Her long hair is wet and freshly combed back from her sculpted cheeks and dimpled chin. Big green eyes twinkle when she smiles. She's wrapped in only a towel. "You look good enough to eat." She winks. "It sucks I've got this stupid headache. Any chance I could talk you into going to the store to get me some BC?"

I try to stifle the cringe. Whenever I think of BC, it brings back the bitter taste of the powder my mother used to make me drink when I had a fever. I look at my beautiful young lover and wonder again why she chooses such an old-fashioned pain remedy. I can't deny her anything though, so I give her a quick peck on the cheek and head back out into the heat.

In under a half hour I'm back at the house, once again parking in the garage. The sun has gone down and the temperature has dropped to a tolerable degree. I turn off the ignition as the garage door slides closed and I'm surprised to see the flash of blue lights. Before I can turn around I hear a firm, authoritative voice. "Step out of the car and place your hands on the roof of the vehicle."

I get out and start to turn around, but the commanding voice stops me again. "Eyes forward. Hands on the roof."

There's something familiar in the voice. It sounds like Jaz, but it's a different Jaz. This Jaz sounds like she belongs in an action movie where she's the badass female hero. *I don't know where this is going, but I'm dying to find out,* I think as I follow orders.

I hear the light thud of boots on the cement floor. A moment later she's close behind me. Her boot taps the inside of my heel. "Spread."

"Jaz, what are you—?"

"Do you want to add resisting arrest to your charges?" she barks, cutting me off.

"Charges?" I barely stifle the urge to chuckle while spreading my legs wider.

Her warm breath on the back of my neck and the feel of her gloved hands on my shoulders make me forget any other questions or protests. A shudder runs through me the moment her hands begin their exploration. I'm so wet, with my legs parted, I know she must smell my desire.

Her hands slide over my back and down past my ass to my thighs. My stockings and her leather gloves make it impossible for skin-to-skin contact, but I'm still so turned on my legs are weak. She presses against me from behind. Her tits are firm against my shoulder blades at the same time as her hands come forward and she cups my breasts.

I can't stifle a groan. The urge to reach back and pull her to me is driving me mad. My hands move toward her, but she backs out of reach.

"Stay still or I'll have to cuff you."

There's an idea with real potential.

She comes forward again. The warmth of her body adds to

my heat and we aren't even touching. Then, her full lips brush against my ear sending a chill racing the length of my spine. "Do you want me to cuff you?"

"It might be for the best, Jaz. I don't know how much longer I can control myself. What happened to your headache?"

She gently takes my hands and brings them together behind my back as she explains. "In the course of an investigation it's permissible for an officer of the law to use deception in order to procure a confession."

I give in to the desire to laugh. "So, you lied to me?"

"I had to get you out of the house in order to set the scene." She presses the full length of her heavenly body against me. I tilt my head back on her shoulder and nuzzle her vanilla-scented neck. "Five times," she continues. "I personally have witnessed you either staring hungrily at my uniform, or touching it in what could be considered an inappropriate manner."

Metal touches my wrists and soon they're locked in place between us. When I try to pull them apart I feel something furry and padded. "Jaz, I don't think these are regulation handcuffs."

She laughs softly. The sound is so warm and inviting I can feel myself melting against her. Her hands come around and she's squeezing my breasts. My nipples are erect for her, straining against the bra and my dress.

It isn't easy with the cuffs, but I manage to cup my fingers and stroke her hips and crotch. Her breath quickens. "You first," she says huskily.

Her left hand dips lower, never losing contact as it descends all the way to my thigh. She grasps the hem of my dress and hikes it up to my waist while her other hand is alternating its attention between my breasts. She kisses and sucks my neck. Her mouth is open and I feel her warm tongue glide along my skin until she reaches my dress's zipper. With her hands busy driving me to a frenzy, it has to be her teeth she's using to lower my zipper halfway to my ass.

"Please." I gasp out the word when her fingers slip inside the band of my underwear. The warm leather of her glove feels so foreign and somehow intensely erotic. She explores me in slow, deliberate patterns. I buck against her and am rewarded with her own gasp when my ass rubs hard against her center.

The sweet pressure builds. My head feels lighter. I can think of only one thing as her fingers press and slide. I look back over my shoulder and her lips crash into mine.

She slips her thigh between mine. One hand is wrapped around my waist while her other plays me like a weeping guitar. I grasp her shirt and pull frantically, but with the cuffs I'm barely able to just pull it from her tight pants.

It feels like something is tearing inside me. Tearing and then mending itself so it's even better than before. My insides quiver, just like my thighs.

She waits until I've caught my breath before she gently turns me around, so I'm finally facing her. She raises her gloved hand, the one that just gave me an incredible orgasm, and caresses her lips. She takes a deep breath, and then slowly slides a finger inside her mouth. She starts to withdraw the finger, but stops and bites the tip.

I inhale a shaky breath. My cheeks are flushed. Blood blazes through my veins. Every pulse point is hammering for attention. My clit still aches for her. I've come undone. I regret my playful agreement earlier about the handcuffs. I'm consumed with want.

She smiles around the glove tip still just barely in her mouth. Her hand slowly pulls free, revealing her manicured fingers. Wavy blonde hair frames her model's face. Hooded eyes, darker from her need, meet mine. There's a current running between us. Its steady thrum draws us closer.

I shake my hands behind me so the metal bracelets jangle. "Get these fucking things off me."

"Wow," she laughs. The delicious sound is low and throaty.

"Take it easy. There's a quick-release button. Feel for it with your thumb."

"I've got other things I want to feel with my thumb."

Her smile is wicked and laced with promises I know she'll have no trouble delivering. She backs up another step. Her fingertips are brushing over the buttons of her crisply starched shirt. She starts to undo one.

My heart races at the sight. I want to be the one to do that. For toy handcuffs, the damn things are unusually strong. No matter how much I pull and twist, they remain in place. I whimper in frustration until I finally remember what she said about the release button. I thumb it over and sigh in relief at my newfound freedom.

I lunge for her. She's too fast. Agile. Soft laughter drifts on the heated air as she dodges my hands and goes inside the house.

I release my other hand from the cuff and finish removing my dress; I don't want to fall and break my neck before I get to give her what we both want. I take off the heels, but leave the stockings on. I think they have the same effect on her that her uniform has on me.

She's in the kitchen when I find her. Her back is to me as she pours red wine into a glass. "Thought you might have worked up a thirst," she says with a grin when she turns to face me.

I take the offered glass and set it beside hers before I catch her silky blonde hair in my fist and tilt her head back. "I'm thirsty for something else," I say against her lips and claim them in a kiss packed with heat and need.

Jaz moans into my mouth, her tongue battling mine as we deepen the kiss, her strong hands roaming freely over my body.

I blindly drag my hands from her hair, mapping my way across her shoulders and the swell of her breasts until I reach the buttons. As much as I love her in this uniform I'm dying to get it off. Her insistent tongue and my own urgency have my fingers fumbling, but I finally get the buttons undone.

With a great deal of effort, I back away from her. I have to see her. She arches under my touch when I trail my finger from her collarbone to her waist. The shirt falls open, revealing firm breasts and taut abs. The steady rise and fall of her gorgeous chest quickens under my gaze. She starts to shrug the rest of the way out of her shirt, but I shake my head. "Please, not yet."

Her cocky grin falls back into place. "You've got it bad for this uniform, don't you?"

I don't answer with words. Instead, I drop to my knees in front of her. My hands are much more adept at unfastening her belt since I can actually see what I'm doing now. *Turnabout is fair play*, I reason. Once the snap on her pants is unfastened, I tug on the zipper with my teeth. My hands grasp the waistband of her pants. Quickly, I pull them, and her thong, to the tops of her boots.

Her fingers twist through my hair as she urges me closer. Sounds of want drift out on her shallow breaths.

There's a bright pink-and-red tattoo of a rose on her left hip. Her pussy, when spread under my thumbs, matches the colors of the ink. I wonder if she or the artist chose the color. If it was the artist, then I think he or she must have chosen it to compliment her. The outer petals start off a light, creamy pink and gradually intensify to hot crimson.

She is wet and inviting. Her scent, an intoxicating blend of musk, vanilla and honey makes me want nothing more than to devour her. "So beautiful," I whisper against her clit, and she trembles. I give her a long lick with the flat of my tongue. Her grip on my hair tightens, her thighs fidget and despite the boots and the pants still at her knees, she spreads wider.

I alternate between long, leisurely licks and fast, hard flicks. Each new moan and gasp from her beautiful mouth spurs me on. Her knees begin to bend. The counter at her back and the hand she now has on my shoulder are the only things keeping her upright.

She makes me so greedy. I want to drink every drop of her, my tongue pressing and sucking. I lick her from her entrance to her clit and back again, laving every inch of her folds until she's bucking and out of control.

"Fingers, babe. Now," she pants her command.

I obey quickly. She's hot and wet enough that I'm sure I don't need to, but I lick two fingers just to be sure. Her pink velvet walls are a perfect fit. She grinds her hips and meets me thrust for needy thrust, my lips back on her hard nub.

"Fuck, fuck, fuck!" Each one she utters is louder than the last. "Yes, god, oh fuck, yes!" She's screaming now.

I love that she doesn't hold back. I suck and fuck her harder until I feel every one of her muscles tighten. Her back goes ramrod straight. For a moment, the only thing moving is her clit as it throbs against my tongue. I'm lost in her flood. I happily lap every bit until she is strong enough to stand on her own.

"Holy shit, babe. That was…" She trails off, her hand in my hair no longer on the verge of pulling out a handful. Her fingers are massaging me gently as she nudges me to stand and look at her. "Fuck, babe. That was amazing. I should arrest you more often."

"Yes, please." I grab the lapels of her shirt and pull her in for a slow, deep kiss. A long while later we drift apart, and I remember something important. "Hey, you didn't even read me my rights."

"Next time," she smiles. "I can't give it all up in one night. I want you to have something to look forward to."

"I look forward to every minute with you," I say truthfully. "But I still think I should know my rights."

"Okay," she says, spinning us in one swift move. Her hands grip my ass and she lifts me onto the counter. "You have the right to remain naked. Anything you say can and will be held against you." She smirks. "So please say, 'hot lesbian cop.'"

MOTHER TONGUE

Camille Duvall

The elaborate writing on our café window proclaims FINEST ITALIAN ICE CREAM. Our recipe is a closely guarded family secret. Café Bianchi is a Belfast landmark, situated on a leafy tree-lined avenue in the south of the city near the University Quarter. What we sell never goes out of fashion; we've been feeding the locals, students and tourists for three decades. There's always a queue for our pizza and if you're lucky, you might be able to grab a table—there are only four of them—and have a sit-down meal. Red leather seats, Formica tabletops and pictures of Italian sunsets and Roman ruins clutter the walls. Mama once had a notion to give the café a makeover but Papa wouldn't hear of it. He was right; the place has an authenticity that comes only with the passing of time.

Last night I dreamt in Italian again. What a strange yet welcome occurrence after all these years. I felt light-headed yet serene as I went about my business this morning, the residue of the dream floating inside me, making me wistful and longing for the sea. I think it might be because I saw Susan on yesterday's news. She was standing in the ancient quad of Queen's University, shaking hands with another dignitary, having been made an honorary doctor of literature. She was radiantly regal in her academic's gown, beaming with pride. Her hair looked as dark and lustrous as it did thirty years ago; mine has long since lost its copper hues. Even if the reporter hadn't said her name, I would still have recognized the sideways tilt of the head that preceded her mischievous peal of laughter.

Susan had been just another customer who liked to hang out at Bianchi's, but then she began to frequent the café on a regular basis. She was from Swallow Bay, a small seaside town about thirty miles along the coast. When she addressed us in Italian one day, we discovered that she studied languages at Queen's, the country's most prestigious seat of learning. Perhaps it was this knowledge combined with her ink-black hair, dark eyes and olive skin that endeared her to my father. Papa warmed to her instantly, calling her Bella Susanna and kissing her hand in an over-the-top chivalrous fashion. Susan responded in kind, but she always did so in such a comical manner that it was impossible to take her seriously. It felt like a silly game, a merry dance that was acted out the moment she entered the café and concluded as she said her goodbyes. I also knew Mama didn't take her seriously. She used to frown and tut-tut but she did this with a twinkle in her eye. It was when I stole glances at Susan only to find her watching me that I began to suspect her real motive for spending so much time with us.

"Rina is an unusual name. Is it short for anything?" We were seated at one of our tiny tables during a quiet spell. Papa was outside the shop, smoking and joking with the other business owners on our street. Mama was upstairs in bed with a migraine.

"Carina."

Susan's dark orbs gleamed at me. I blushed. She smiled.

"So, you're telling me that your full name is Carina, Italian for 'little darling'?"

I nodded and Susan tilted her head, assessing me. I blushed again. Out came her slow smile again.

"It's beautiful."

"Rina is b-b-better."

"No it is not. I'm going to call you Carina, *mi Carina*."

I knew then for certain, when she called me her little darling, I hadn't been imagining things, she did like me. Right now, she was looking at me intently and I was held captive by her, mesmerized. But then the spell was broken when a customer entered and I had to take his order.

I was eighteen when we settled in Belfast, and Italian was my mother tongue, but within six months I spoke fluent English. Fluent in my head but not always when I spoke. For when I was nervous or under pressure my words trembled out in a stumbling gush. It didn't help that my father mocked my stutter in private: "Caca-carina B-b-bianchi. Don't speak with the customers Rina, the ice cream will have melted by the time you finish a sentence!" It is one of many things for which I will never forgive him. Nowadays, I can say my name with a flourish and take pride in what it means to others: Carina Bianchi, owner and managing director of Bianchi's, the United Kingdom's favorite ice cream.

Whenever Susan was around, I got to speak Italian. She said it was helping her studies and Papa was delighted the *estudiosa* had chosen us. To listeners we probably sounded like a stereotypical Italian family with our boisterous, rapid-fire chat; the splendid rat-tat-tatting of mock incredulity when something deliberately outrageous provoked debate. At first, I watched these exchanges wishing I could join in, but I didn't have the nerve. I was easily tongue-tied and despite Susan's attempts to include me I would blush and shake my head no. I would smile and roll my eyes, enjoying the spectacle as this vibrant woman ran linguistic rings around my father. I was just happy to have her near. When Susan was in the café, the workload felt less like a captive burden, the heat from the huge pizza oven not so furnace-like. Papa would joke with customers, smile at Mama, and his monosyllabic interactions with me would take a backseat. But as time wore on, I started to contribute, encouraged by Susan—she was so persistent. Papa didn't appear to notice. In fact, it was probably the only time he didn't make some wisecrack about my stammer, because when I spoke Italian I did so fluently and unbrokenly.

I was smitten. How transparent I must have been; I felt so awkward and ungainly around Susan, around the lithe gracefulness of her. How could someone like me think I could ever be with someone like her? If I wasn't torturing myself wondering if she really did like me or if she was merely playing with me, then I was spending sleepless nights in my sweat-drenched bed imagining what making love with her would be like. My imagination was vivid but limited. I had never been kissed thanks to the watchful eye of an overprotective father. And so while my fantasies allowed me to indulge in what it might be like to let my fingers caress her skin, to experience the sensation of her full lips on mine, or what it would feel like to take her breast in my mouth, I would have to stop short, unsure of what to do next. My fitful, fantasy-driven sleep would leave me exhausted and frustrated. I had lived a sheltered life in Italy and now in Belfast my existence was limited to the café; back then the boundaries of my world were small and tight and closed. Airless and graceless. Just a few hundred yards away was the university, where people from all over the world came to study. I knew Susan would allow me a glimpse into that world and one day lead me to its doors.

Mama was a kind, peaceful woman, but she suffered from depression, no doubt exacerbated by marriage to a domineering husband. She was often powerless to protect me from his cruel taunts; he simply ignored her. My stutter infuriated him and he used it to taunt me mercilessly. He would complain that I didn't have his business acumen or I lacked his natural flair with customers. I was consigned to the pizza oven, sweltering in silence at the café's coalface, while he played the gregarious Italian for our customers. I know now that there was nothing I could ever have done to please him. I was the only child to come from his loins and the daughter he never wanted.

When Susan suggested she take her Italian lessons up a notch, beginning with the two of us visiting the local art galleries and museums, my father didn't object. He probably didn't want her to think he was impolite and he had to agree with her that the world didn't revolve around politics and football. Spending time with Susan away from the café was bliss. We visited galleries and museums where she would regale me with the sordid details of the tortured artists' scandalous lives, but more often we would find little coffeehouses off the beaten track to sit and while away an afternoon.

"Let's speak in English," she said.

My eyebrows danced in surprise. Susan had been insistent that I never let her speak anything but Italian when we were together.

"Whatever you wish, Susan. I think, perhaps, you have tired of my mother tongue?" I was trying my best to be cavalier.

"I could never tire of it. Or you, *mi Carina.*"

Mi Carina. It got me every time. I blushed—so much for my cavalier attitude. I watched Susan as her eyes followed the scarlet flush that spread from my face to my throat. Then her eyes met mine. She tilted her head and smiled mischievously.

"You are evil, Susan." I laughed.

"You are beautiful, Carina. Accept the compliment for once. Please?"

"Stop it."

"Why? I'm only stating the facts. You have the most exquisite green eyes and your beautiful red hair makes you look more Irish than me." She paused for a moment, drinking me in. "And that skin of yours, it's like porcelain. I can only imagine how smooth it is to the touch." She reached across the table and took my hand, but I pulled it away. She looked hurt. We sat in silence, Susan staring out of the window, me fiddling with my spoon as my brain raced frantically for something to say.

I took a sip of coffee and pulled a face. "This stuff is foul."

"I know. Isn't it criminal that we actually paid for this?" She smiled then and the atmosphere around our little bubble improved instantly.

"We have gallons of great-tasting coffee back at the café," I offered, "free for the likes of us."

Susan's face clouded over. "Why do you let him treat you like dirt? I hate it."

This had become a familiar talking point. I was routinely quizzed about why my father got away with being so harsh with me.

"It's just the way it is. He's my father, I have to respect him."

"He's a bully who doesn't deserve your respect. He'll never earn mine."

"Why then do you act like he's so great? You spend most of your time cracking jokes with him, talking nonsense about football. In fact, you spend more time at Bianchi's than you do in class."

"Because I put on a good act of letting him think he's Mister Wonderful. I can't stand the man. I'm sorry Carina, I know he's your father but he's holding you back. You should be out in the world, doing something, anything, that pleases you." She ran her fingers through her hair. "And I spend time at the café because it means I get to see you. Even when I have to spend time in his company, I manage because I know you're near." She leaned forward in her seat. "I've said too much. I'm sorry."

"It's okay," I said. "I know you're right, but for now there's nothing I can do. Don't ever let Papa hear you talking like that."

"Don't fear, I won't. And while we're on the subject of talking, have you noticed anything?"

I shook my head, puzzled. "No. What?"

"*Mi Carina,* your stammer is gone." Susan took my hand and this time I didn't pull away; I felt her strength and confidence surge through me like an electrical bolt.

The heat wave that had the city sweltering for weeks offered a welcome hiatus one Thursday afternoon when overcast skies threatened to bring summer to an abrupt end. It seemed to suit my mood. Susan had graduated several weeks earlier, coming top of her class. In two days she would be en route to America to join her family's annual vacation. She breezed into the café with her customary flamboyance and conducted her ritual with my father. But then she whispered to me in a quick, hushed voice too low for Papa to hear, "It's time I took you to Swallow Bay. Grab your shades and an umbrella, you'll probably need both." She turned then to address my father and told him she was taking me to meet her family. He wasn't to know that they had already left the country, but the surprised look on Papa's face was priceless, his eyebrows rising into his hairline at the thought of anyone wanting to introduce me to their family. He had no time to find reasons to keep me in the café that day. Susan and I exited as quickly as we could, leaving a thunder-faced Papa in our wake.

We took the train from Botanic station. Susan sat next to me and held my hand. She arranged her jacket so as to conceal our interlocking fingers. I remember her soft, delicate hands; the calmness that enveloped me the moment I touched her smooth skin.

Susan took me to a small stretch of beach that only she knew about. It wasn't immediately visible and it required determination to make the fifteen-minute hike across jutting rocks before the little cove revealed itself. The journey was worth it. The pale white sand covered only a few meters before it met the clear blue water. We were surrounded by the jutting shoreline, protected from prying eyes. I knew I was venturing into uncharted waters.

Susan began to take off her clothes. I stood motionless. She realized I hadn't moved. "What are you waiting for? Get a move on before it starts to rain!"

I was shocked into action. "Are you out of your mind? We've no swimwear."

"You don't need it. Come on. Just imagine you're back in Puglia and you need to cool off." She ran then, naked, into the water. It's no lie that I was curious to see what her body looked like. I had already guessed from the clothes she wore and her contours that her build was slim and boyish. I wasn't shy about exposing my own nakedness; I knew I was well defined. I had inherited my mother's genes and never gained weight. I suppose it helped that I didn't succumb to the café's diet of pizza and ice cream. I joined her in the water. Could it have been warm? I don't remember.

I tried not to stare at Susan's breasts. Her nipples poked out defiantly above the water. She caught me looking. "I know they're small," she grinned, "but they're perfectly formed. And you know what they say?"

"No, tell me, what do they say?"

"Anything more than a handful is a waste!"

We dried ourselves with our clothes and lay on the sand to let the weak sun do the rest. It was getting cold, but I didn't care. I had never had such unguarded access to her before, such space and time to linger over her. My gaze followed the length of her body, taking in her long, toned limbs and flat belly, the small breasts and graceful neck. When my eyes traveled to her face I found her looking at me intently. I looked away, but then gradually my eyes journeyed back to hers and there she was, gazing at me, smiling.

"You look happy, *mi Carina.*"

"I am. I am exquisitely happy."

"Why?"

"I don't know why. It's probably spending time in the water. I miss it."

She sighed then. I searched her face. "What is it?"

"Give me something to work with here." Susan was being playful but I knew she found me exasperating.

"Okay. I'm happy because I'm with you."

"At last. A declaration!"

"Of sorts," I added. I couldn't help it.

"Of sorts? A compliment followed by a retraction of aforementioned compliment. Cheers, Carina."

"Don't be like that, Susan. Just as we're getting close, you're leaving. Anyway, I might even like men. Who knows?"

"Who are you trying to kid, *mi Carina?* You're into me and I'm into you. Fact. That's why we're here today, to do something about it. Then we can plan how to spring you from your Papa's prison. Let's get dressed, we're going to my house."

I had never been kissed before that day, had never been intimate with another human being. Many women have come and gone in my life but the experience of that afternoon has never been bettered. We barely spoke during the twenty-minute walk to Susan's house. Once inside, we went straight to her room. She asked me if I would like some water and I shook my head. She put her arms out and drew me into her and began to slowly undress me. At first I didn't know how to react, but the heat rising inside me took over and I followed Susan's lead, unbuttoning her shirt, unbuckling her belt. Soon we were tearing off each other's clothes, kissing, biting and licking as we tumbled naked into the bed.

Susan tenderly stroked my body. I responded, gently flicking her nipples as she caressed my breasts. I felt Susan's tongue begin its slow descent. When she nibbled and licked me I gasped with surprise; her probing tongue unleashed sensations I never knew existed until then. I thought I would explode as Susan expertly drank in my juices, causing me to almost faint with desire as my nerve endings reached a crescendo. I came, my back arching involuntarily, and as I struggled to get my breath back, when I thought it was over, Susan's fingers slipped inside me, finding purchase in the hot wetness. Again my body responded, wave after convulsing wave of pleasure before the final release.

Susan held me in her arms as my heartbeat resumed its normal pace.

Feeling bold, encouraged, I kissed Susan hungrily; I could taste my sweet juices on her lips, and the passion rose in us again. My efforts became more urgent as I mounted her. I wasn't sure what came next, but instinct told me that I was on the right track; it was as if we were meant to fit together, the wetness and friction melding as one. Our bodies rode together, the intensity of the motion driving me wild. Susan's breathing rasped. She groaned aloud as she begged me to take her. I was amazed by what was happening; this woman was in ecstasy beneath me. My confidence grew and I bit into Susan's neck as she juddered and screamed out her orgasm.

I will never forget the sweat-soaked sheets as I went down on Susan for the first time. My tongue probed as I plunged my fingers inside her, feeling the swell of her as her thighs began to tremble. She began to pant out my name to the rhythm of my fingers, faster and faster. Then, for a moment she was silent as her head snapped back on the pillow. I thought something was wrong until she emitted a howl as another orgasm revealed itself.

Later as we lay in each other's arms, I murmured a thank-you. She laughed and sighed contentedly. "It's me who should be thanking you. I just knew you were a natural."

When we got back to Belfast, Susan insisted on walking me to the café. It was late and the entrance to the apartment was via a secluded alleyway. She wanted to come in to talk to my parents about me joining her family vacation, but I wouldn't allow it. I was afraid they would see how everything had changed between Susan and me. She promised to come to the café the next day and then kissed me good night. The kiss was swift and chaste;

we had to be careful, but our tight embrace betrayed our true intentions. We heard a foot scrape some loose stones. It was my father. I don't know how long he had been standing there, what he had heard or seen. Susan opened her mouth to speak but he was upon us in one motion, sweeping her aside and shoving open the apartment door. He threw me inside, a snarl of disgust on his lips. He manhandled Susan along the alley, and I heard her protest that if he didn't let her go she would call the police. That was July 1986. Susan and I have not seen or spoken to each other since that night.

That's how I've come to be in Swallow Bay today, led by memories almost thirty years old. I don't know if Susan's family still live here, it's just the place where everything finally came right before it unraveled again. For all I know, Susan flew in for her graduation and is on a plane on her way back home. It would be nice to think that she would have called into Café Bianchi. She might even be there right now. If she is, then she will find it just as she left it, the décor intact and now fashionably retro-chic. The young staff are not Italian but the produce is. If she asks about me, they will tell her that I no longer work in the café but manage the ice cream side of the business, overseeing the ever-expanding Bianchi brand. But she probably won't do any of this. Why would she? She has probably forgotten all about me. I wish I knew more about her. The dust jackets of every one of her novels offer the same maddeningly scant information: born in Swallow Bay, educated at the Queen's University of Belfast and resident of Puglia.

Puglia. That's the bit that breaks my heart, to know that Susan lives in the town where I was born and lived until I left for Ireland. I'd love to know why she chose there of all places. She doesn't use social media, I've checked. Perhaps I could write to her via her publisher, but what would I say? I would want to know why she disappeared from my life and what part my father played in it. I never knew what he said to her that night, what threats were made. She never came back to the café, or if she did then we were deliberately kept apart. I know now that I should have acted differently that night. I reacted with a misplaced, unnecessary guilt, and it revealed itself to my father just enough for him to use it to shame me into submission.

Over the next days, weeks and months, he bombarded me with insults, and my poor mother's depression meant she was powerless to challenge him. It was when he resorted to one of his old taunts that I finally found the key to my liberation.

"D-d-d-dyke. You're a bloody d-d-d-dyke!"

I slapped him. Once, hard. In the few moments that he was shocked into silence the scales were lifted from my eyes.

"Are you jealous, Papa? Jealous that she wanted me and not you? That's the last time you will ever goad me about who or what I am. And you will never again mock how I speak."

I never spoke to my father again. He lived for another few years but by then I had been to university and earned my business degree. I inherited the café when Mama died and I began to transform the Bianchi name into a major ice-cream brand.

I return to the city, to a beautiful summer's afternoon brimming with promise. I decide to pay Café Bianchi a visit. I stroll down the leafy tree-lined avenue, thinking of the times when Susan walked beside me. Her life force had brought opportunity and light into my dull little world. Perhaps I *will* write to her publisher, what harm could it do? It would be good to meet her again, to sit and talk in my mother tongue; to acknowledge the wonderful changes she brought to my life. When I enter the café, the young waiter beams at me from behind the counter.

"Hi, Miss Bianchi."

"Hi, Steve. How's business today?"

"Splendid as always. Here, I have something for you."

I watch as he reaches behind him to lift an envelope from the shelf. He turns and hands it to me. "I didn't know you had such famous friends."

I stare at him for a moment as his words sink in. I nod, barely able to speak.

I take the envelope to one of the little tables and sit down.

Steve goes back to his duties. I turn the blank envelope over and over in my hands; it could be meant for anyone. I open it. Inside is a single sheet of paper. I recognize the flamboyant scrawl. It begins: *Mi Carina...*

PLEDGE NIGHT

Radclyffe

"Are you sure you want to do this?" I asked Kari for probably
the hundredth time in the last hour. The whole thing had seemed
like such a good idea until I really thought about what it meant
for a straight girl to pledge a lesbian sorority, even though the
sorority made a point of being open to all. If that was true, why
was the initiation so secret? I mean, like cloak-and-dagger secret.
Tonight was the official pledge night, and we didn't know where
we were going, who would be there or what would happen.
What if Kari hated whatever it was that was coming? No pun
intended.

Kari slammed her hands on her size 1 gymnast hips and
gave me the evil eye. Her coffee-and-cream complexion always
flushed to a lovely cocoa color when she was pissed. She looked
ready for whipped cream and chocolate shavings right about
now. "How many times do I have to tell you, I'll be fine. It's not
like I don't know what you get up to in bed. You've been telling
me since we were fifteen."

Well, yeah, okay. That's what best friends did, right, shared the highs and lows of high school dating, including the sex and broken hearts? Besides, Kari knew about the first girl I ever had a crush on—her. We'd gotten as far as kissing a few times before she let me down easy.

"You're a great kisser," she'd told me when we were lying on top of my covers fully clothed one night after soccer practice. We'd been practicing kissing for a couple of weeks, and I spent a lot of time fantasizing about what happened next. I hadn't gotten to try any of the scenarios I'd fantasized about yet, but Kari had always been able to read me really well and knew what I was picturing. "But you know," she said, "I don't think I want you to be my girlfriend."

My heart felt like applesauce in my chest, crushed and pulpy. I didn't say anything because if I opened my mouth I'd probably make embarrassing whimpering sounds.

She kissed me again, gently, sweetly. "You're my best friend, and I bet if we had sex, it would be amazing. I'm pretty sure I'm bi for you, but the rest of the time, not so much, and you know—I kind of like the wanting part best."

Weirdly, that seemed to make it okay. She wanted me, and I knew she'd always love me. Ditto for me, and here we were. Best friends and still hot for each other.

I studied her annoyed and totally gorgeous face. She had almond-shaped dark eyes, high slanted cheekbones and a wide sensuous mouth. She was movie-star beautiful, at least I'd always thought so. "You're not just pledging because you love me?"

She tried to keep looking mad, but she burst out laughing. "I think it'll be a trip for us to be in that sorority together. Everybody knows it's a cool place to be. And yeah, I *do* like being where you are." She gave me a little hip bump. "You're such a dork, and I don't trust you by yourself."

I laughed. She knew all about my romantic foibles and failures and near disasters over the years. But hey, now I was almost nineteen and experienced. Mature. Totally unprepared for whatever was coming. I took her hand and mumbled, "I think I'd be scared out of my pants to do this without you."

She gave my hand a little tug and sent me a pretend kiss. "Honey, you're going to be out of your pants one way or the other tonight."

My throat was dry. "Yeah, I think that might be what I'm afraid of."

"Well, you're the lesbian. You ought to know what it's all about."

"That's the whole point of the initiation. No one knows what it's all about—at least no one who will talk about it. All I know is, we have to go through this step in order to finalize our pledge."

"Right," Kari said, "it's like a hazing, but they don't call it that. It's a rite of passage. They probably make us… You know," she said with a questioning lilt in her voice, "I don't actually have any idea what they might do."

"Or have us do," I muttered.

"I guess we'll find out soon." Kari glanced at her watch. "Because they're supposed to pick us up right about—"

On cue, a knock sounded at the door of the dorm room we shared.

I opened it and two women, one dark and one light, one brown eyed, one blue, stood shoulder to shoulder filling the frame. The blonde's slightly curly hair was down to her shoulders, and she wore an aqua-blue dress that hugged her curvy body, plunged between her breasts and ended just barely south of her ass. The brunette, taller and slimmer than the bombshell blonde, looked dangerously debonair in a black tuxedo shirt, black belt and tailored black silk trousers. Our ushers for the evening.

The blonde smiled at me, her blue eyes frankly appraising. "Larson?"

I nodded, found my voice. "Yes."

"I'm Shar."

Kari came up beside me and, like she often did, rested her hand on the small of my back, answering sweetly to save me further humiliation. "Hi. I'm Kari."

The brunette took Kari's free hand, raised it to her mouth and kissed her knuckles. "Hello." Her voice was buttery smooth, rich and deep. "I'm Paulie. I'll be your guide tonight."

I waited for Kari's response. She could still back out. I wouldn't blame her. The whole idea was probably crazy to begin with.

Kari hooked her fingers around Paulie's forearm and stepped up beside her. "I can't wait to get started."

We followed Shar and Paulie into the elevator and rode silently down to the lobby and out into the parking lot. We buckled up, slid on blindfolds, and someone started the engine.

When we parked, Shar told us we could remove the blindfolds. "Let's go, lovelies," she said.

Kari and I followed the two sorority sisters down the ramp and into the boathouse. I was surprised to see at least a dozen other women, some of whom I knew by name, others only by sight, already gathered in a loose group in the center of the big space. I recognized six of the senior sorority sisters in addition to our ushers. I counted the pledges again. There were sixteen of us. A two-to-one ratio. I wondered if that meant anything.

Sorority president Rainer McDaniels stepped to the center of the darkened boathouse situated on the large lake that bordered our campus, and the low murmur of conversation between the sorority sisters abruptly stopped. The rest of us had been silent, probably too scared to speak, and a hush fell over the room. Rainer was legendary on campus. A senior now, she was some kind of musical prodigy and could have had a career in classical music, but had decided to pursue a high-level tech engineering degree, the details of which I could barely understand. Pale and lean, dark-haired and black-eyed, she was the epitome of a brooding genius.

"Tonight," Rainer pronounced, "we finalize our list of pledges and offer you the opportunity to join us in solidarity and seduction for the remainder of your time. I'll remind you that everyone has signed an oath of secrecy, and even those of you who will not become one of us are sworn to uphold that vow." She didn't smile even though her tone was soft and seductive. "Just remember this. If you ever decide to share what happens here tonight," she said, glancing around, and it seemed as if she made eye contact with each of the pledges, "we'll know. We'll know, and we will uphold the honor of the oath. Do you all understand?"

"Yes," we answered in one voice. I glanced out of the corner of my eye at Kari. She was staring, an odd expression on her face. If I had to put a name to it, I'd say she was fascinated. Maybe she really would enjoy what was coming.

"Good." Rainer smiled. "We want tonight to be pleasurable for all of you, even those of you who will be eliminated."

I registered the shock on everyone's face and was sure my expression echoed it. What did that mean, elimination?

"We've invited twice as many participants as we plan to accept as new pledges. All of you show the kind of personality and passion we seek, but we can only make a final decision after we see how you put that potential into practice." Someone pushed a large green fabric chair into the circle and Rainer sat down, resting her hands on the broad wooden arms and crossing one ankle over the other. The other sorority members came to stand on either side of her. I was viewing the queen, or in this case, the king, and the royal court.

Two sorority members brought maroon velvet-covered foot-stools, placed them on either side of Rainer's chair and knelt on them, facing each other with Rainer in the middle. One unbuttoned Rainer's shirt while the other opened the tab on her trousers and slid down the zipper. Rainer's expression didn't change. She looked as if she wasn't even aware of what was happening.

"For the first elimination," Rainer said, "each of you will turn to your left and face the person beside you. She will be your partner."

My partner was a small Asian woman whom I remembered seeing at rush week but never spoke to. Her eyes were cool and assured, although not unfriendly.

"Each pair will retire to the furniture provided. Before you recline, please remove all your clothing."

Someone laughed. Nervous laughter.

"Please begin."

For a second, neither of us moved. Min, whose name I finally remembered, suddenly swiveled and strode to a broad hunter-green sofa ten feet away, directly in front of Rainer. She pulled her sweater off over her head, just as quickly divested herself of her bra, and then pushed her jeans and underwear down and kicked off her shoes. She was naked before I'd managed to follow her. My hands shook as I unbuttoned my shirt, pulled it from my jeans, and, working on autopilot, continued to disrobe. I sensed Kari somewhere close behind me, a soothing presence. Whatever craziness was about to begin, I wasn't alone.

"You and your partner are to pleasure each other simultaneously, using your mouth, hands or tongue. The first member of each couple to orgasm will be eliminated. You may start now."

I caught glimpses of the two attendants on either side of Rainer stroking her exposed breasts and abdomen. She was superhot, but I didn't have a chance to watch. I stared at Min, wondering which of us would bolt for the door first.

"I'd like the top, if you don't mind." She smiled, a disconcertingly self-possessed smile. "I'm sure this won't take long."

She was obviously confident. Well, so was I.

"Sure." I stretched out on the sofa, pulled a small throw pillow behind my head so I knew the angle would be good, and let my legs fall open. She deftly straddled me, her knees at my shoulder level, her elbows beside my hips, her arms cradling my legs from underneath. If there was a bell to start, I didn't hear it. Her mouth was on me before I'd barely gotten comfortable between her thighs. My hips jerked and I swear she laughed. I wrapped my arms around her ass and tried not to think about who was watching. Min knew what she was doing. She started out licking on either side of my clit, just enough pressure to make me hard, and ending lower down, stroking the sensitive lining of my inner lips. My clit twitched and pulsed. She was good, sure, but so was I.

I grabbed her ass to keep her from pulling away and closed my mouth around her whole pussy, sucking gently. Her clit was right at the level of my tongue and I sucked it between small, quick flicks on the underside. Her thighs trembled but she made no sound. She didn't have to. She liked it.

Concentrating on her helped me ignore the growing pressure between my legs. If I could keep my mind on what I was doing to her, I might not come all over her face. When she reached down and stroked my opening with two fingers, I wasn't quite so sure. My clit pounded. A hard ball of heat grew and throbbed in my pussy, threatening to explode. I wanted to be stroked, to be filled, to be fucked while she sucked me. I wanted to come in her mouth, all over her. Fuck. I was losing my rhythm, and she moved in for the kill. Her tongue was a magic wand, stroking, teasing, pressing. I was going to come so fucking hard.

I moaned, tensed my ass and tried to pull away, but she held fast, sucking the shaft between her lips so I couldn't escape.

I had to distract her, or I'd be eliminated very, very quickly. She was disciplined, but I knew she wanted to come—I could tell from the turgid fullness of her clit, the way her pussy lips opened and slicked. Her thighs trembled, and I knew I had her on the edge. Trouble was, she had me there too. My clit was ready to go off in another ten seconds no matter what I did. I slid a finger inside and fucked her while I licked her, but I still couldn't get her to go. I was going to lose the damn competition, and if I did, I might end up leaving Kari there alone. I couldn't do that.

I felt the churning, pulsing blast building inside me, and desperate, I tried the only thing I hadn't tried yet. I ran my thumb between her lips, soaking up her come, and pressed it to her ass, circling and massaging the tight ring of muscle while I sucked her clit. Maybe the surprise was what broke her, but she pulled her mouth off my pussy and cried, "No! No, no, no."

I almost cheered. *Oh yes.*

Her pussy pulsed against my face and she came jerking in my arms, writhing against my mouth while her ass clenched over and over. When she finished, limp and moaning with her face buried against my thigh, I dropped my head back, gasping. My clit was still on fire, but I hadn't come. Yet.

Waiting for my body to slide down from the almost-coming brink, I turned my head, searching for Kari. She wasn't far away. She never was. She straddled the lap of a muscular redhead in a big overstuffed chair six feet away. Her back was to me. All I could see were her toned shoulders, the delicate sweep of her spine, and her round muscular ass, rhythmically flexing as she rocked against the woman beneath her. One of the redhead's arms disappeared between their bodies, and I imagined her stroking Kari's clit, sliding her fingertips over Kari's slick pussy, bringing her closer and closer to the edge. Kari jerked, her hips starting to shake. Damn it, she was going to come. Watching her get ready to come pushed me right back up to the brink. Fuck, I had to be careful or I'd come by accident.

I heard a moan and realized it was Kari. *Aw, Kari, come on. Don't let her win.* Just when I was certain Kari was about to come all over the redhead's lap, Kari reached back, cupped the redhead's pussy, and in one sweet move, slipped her fingers inside. I grinned when the redhead's legs shot out, stiff and trembling, and her whole body arched off the chair. I heard a yell, and knew it was all over. Kari did her nicely, fucking her slowly until she finished. You'd never know it was the first time Kari'd ever done it. As the redhead's legs slowly relaxed, Kari looked over her shoulder in my direction. She smirked, and I could almost hear her say, "Not bad for a beginner, huh?"

I gave her a thumbs-up. Smugly, she turned back and kissed the girl. Hell, she'd just topped like a veteran. Apparently, Kari and I were the top tops in the room, since the other couples were all still going at it. Moans, cries, babbling, and curses filled the air. I concentrated on getting my clit back to baseline. Whatever was coming next, I didn't want to start out at half-mast. First Min and then Kari had me wanting to come as bad as I could ever remember.

After another few minutes, Rainer's voice penetrated the haze of sexual murmurings.

"This round has ended. Those of you who have come will no longer be joining us for the rest of the evening. You will be escorted back to your rooms. We thank you for pledging and for joining the evening's entertainment."

One of the younger sisters came to stand by us. Min sighed and gave me a sweet kiss. "Good luck. You were fantastic."

I sat up and pushed my clothes into a pile while she finished dressing. Across from me, Kari did the same. *You all right?* I mouthed.

She grinned. *Super.*

I'd seen her naked before, but somehow, the muted light of the boathouse and knowing she must be as aroused as me made her more beautiful than ever. Her dark nipples, tight and small, stood erect on her perfectly oval breasts. Her lean belly sloped down to muscular thighs and delicate calves. My clit twitched, and I gritted my teeth. Really, really bad timing to be this horny.

As if she was reading my mind, she shook her head in mock disapproval. I could see her eyes laughing. She was enjoying this, for sure.

I jerked when Rainer's voice rang out again.

"We've now reached the final point of elimination. Each of the remaining pledges will please have a seat."

While I'd been ogling Kari, the sorority members had arranged big chairs like Rainer's throne in a semicircle. Eight of them. I glanced at Kari, who lifted a shoulder as if to say, *We've come this far*, and we took seats side by side in the half circle. I didn't know the woman to my left.

She had to be close to six feet tall, with big wide shoulders, a long lean torso and muscular legs. Her skin was ebony and glistening, her breasts as full and tight looking as mine felt. She glanced at me out of almond-shaped eyes similar to Kari's, but she didn't speak. Everyone was on edge.

Rainer walked to the center of the half circle.

"You've all proven your sexual expertise, and for that you will be rewarded. Your only requirement to pass this challenge is to exhibit control and stamina while the sisters take their pleasure. You will refrain from orgasm until each of the sisters has finished. To show you that can be done, I'll join you in this exercise."

The two women who'd flanked her before on the footstools stepped into the circle and quickly undressed her as if they had done it dozens of times before. They probably had. Naked, she settled into the chair facing the semicircle so everyone had a view of what was about to happen. Shar placed the red velvet footstool in front of her and knelt on it. Other sorority members formed a line until one was facing each of us. A brunette—a sophomore, I think—wearing nothing but a slinky black bra, matching lacy panties and a hint of a hungry smile stepped up between my open thighs. Why did she have to hit just about all of my fantasy triggers, like I wasn't hot enough already?

"Begin," Rainer said.

Everyone knelt and my breath whooshed out.

Shar went down on Rainer and, as if at a silent signal, all the others followed suit. I gripped the arm of my chair as a warm mouth closed over me. Out of the corner of my eye, I saw Kari stiffen and I tried really, really hard not to imagine how she must feel right now. I could take it. I'd have to take it. How long could they possibly do this?

My clit tensed and plumped up as the brunette between my thighs teased and sucked me. Okay, if I didn't think about it, didn't look at her, I could do this. I watched Rainer, her expression impassive as the blonde head between her legs slowly moved up and down. I could imagine Shar's tongue sliding between Rainer's pussy lips the way the brunette's slipped over mine. Shar reached up and caressed Rainer's tight belly and breasts, moving from one to the other, thumbs brushing her nipples. Rainer watched me watching her and smiled as if highly amused.

Suddenly the mouth on me pulled away and I breathed a sigh of relief. Okay, I made it. And then the sorority sisters got up as one, moved in a choreographed game of musical chairs, and another woman took the place between my thighs. Jeez. This one's rhythm was totally different, faster, harder, fingertips and tongue dipping inside me and then up and swirling around my clit. The increased tempo jacked me up hard and fast.

Beside me, Kari moaned. My thighs tightened.

"Don't," I gasped, whether an order for Kari or myself I didn't know. Damn if the woman between my legs didn't laugh.

Next to me, the big tough number whimpered. "Fuck, she's gonna make me come."

My vision swam. I was about to come myself. I tried to focus, searching for anything to divert me, and my gaze landed on Rainer again. Her face was set in that same smug expression as if nothing was happening, but I recognized the tension in her body as a redhead this time licked and fucked her. Damn, though, Rainer's control was amazing. I gritted my teeth, met her gaze. If she could hold on, so could I.

Blessedly, whatever timer they could hear must've gone off because they all moved again. How many times were they going to do this? The few seconds when the contact was gone was enough for me to back myself down, but every time my clit twitched, I was closer.

"I don't think I can do this," Kari whispered, her voice ragged and faint. "I want to come so bad."

"Don't," I said, and now Shar was between my legs, parting me, caressing the sides of my clit with her thumbs. I made the mistake of looking down as she licked me. Her eyes met mine, hazy and hot. Oh fuck. "*Fuck!*"

I wrenched my gaze away.

Rainer was chuckling. I grimaced, ground my teeth together. Fuck no. Rainer caressed the back of the head of the woman between her legs, her hips slowly thrusting. Goddamn her, Rainer was fucking her mouth as if she had all the time in the world. I didn't dare try that. If I did, I was going to come in Shar's mouth in a hot second.

The big jock next to me shouted, bucking and writhing in her chair. I couldn't not watch. The sister sucking her off stroked her belly and her breasts until she collapsed, muttering *Fuck fuck fuck* over and over again. I realized I'd cupped Shar's neck, pulling her mouth harder against me, the way I did when I wanted to come. I forced myself to let go. I heard two other pledges come, one keening as if in pain, the other hooting wildly. Whenever someone orgasmed, the sorority sisters who brought them off dropped out of the line. Thank god. Maybe I had a chance to win whatever this game was. They all switched places again, and then only Kari and I were left. Along with Rainer.

Rainer, as cool as ever. Her eyes were hooded, her knuckles white on the edges of the chair, her expression remote and superior.

"I'm going to come this time," Kari groaned. "I have to come so bad I don't care anymore."

Paulie knelt in front of Kari. Shar moved into the space between our chairs and a redhead took her place between my legs. When the redhead slipped inside me and started kissing my clit, Shar reached down and played with my nipples.

"Oh god," Kari cried. "It feels so good. She's gonna make me come."

"Me too," I murmured. Enough already.

Kari reached between us and grabbed my arm. I found her hand and held it. Rainer smiled as if she approved.

My clit was on fire, a pulsing ember between my legs. I had maybe ten seconds to go. And then I saw it. A grimace broke across Rainer's face, and she glanced down at the brunette sucking her. Her stomach muscles tightened, etched beneath her skin like carved engravings on a stone statue. She was about to come. She looked over at me, and I grinned, my vision going dark.

"Now," I called, the sweet lightning coiling up my spine.

Rainer shouted, coming at the same instant, and I felt my body go rigid like I'd been electrocuted. I came and came, Kari's hand still gripped in mine, my eyes locked on Rainer's. Harder than I ever had in my life.

Limp and exhausted, I glanced at Kari.

"Nice job," she gasped, laughing.

Rainer rose, as cool again as if nothing had ever happened. Naked, she passed down the line of pledges, kissing each one, murmuring a welcome. She lingered a minute with Kari and then came to me. Bracing her hands on the arms of my chair, she leaned down, but instead of kissing me, she whispered in my ear, "Next time you come tonight, I'm going to be the one making you scream. No one touches you again until me. Do you think you can take it?"

The answer was easy.

Pledge night was over, but the pleasure was just beginning.

COYOTE GIRL

Evey Brett

She came to me at dusk, a creature as wild as the coyotes and foxes that hunted in the shadows of my little adobe home. One moment, there were only the shadows cast by the stones and mesquite trees, and the next, she emerged, lean and lithe and ghostly with her rifle slung over one shoulder and a kerchief tied in a band around her head. My heart leapt to see her, even as I let out a cry of worry as I saw the blood on the front of her shirt and the way she staggered as she walked. I'd never asked her name. She'd never asked mine. So I called her my *chica coyote*. Coyote Girl. A trickster if ever there was one.

Once, there had been only Apache roaming this part of the Arizona territory. Now, immigrants, prospectors and soldiers traveled along what, until last year, had been the Overland Mail route. Until I'd come here I'd made a good living as a *curandera*, tending to the sick and injured. My mother had taught me the art, just as her mother had taught her, all the way back through the generations, and I'd added to my knowledge by being a nurse to those fighting in the Mexican wars. I'd hoped to teach it to my daughter, with whom I'd been traveling the route in search of a better life, but when she'd been bitten by a rattlesnake, we'd been forced to take shelter just inside the valley. That was how I'd met Coyote Girl. She'd found me weeping over my daughter's grave.

I should have been afraid. Mexicans and Apaches had been at war for years and I was an invader in her land, but my heart was too sore to do anything but stare at the slight, masculine figure that had suddenly appeared. I was tired of losing the battle against death and dying. I could not escape it, even here. *"Mi hija,"* I said, and then added in English, "My daughter."

A look of sympathy crossed her face. She took a pinch of pollen from a pouch at her belt, scattered it over the grave and wailed. Her lament rose and fell like a coyote's howl, giving voice to the grief I could not. At the end, she took my hand and gave it a gentle, comforting squeeze. As quietly as she'd come, she vanished. I rarely saw her, but I would often find coyote paw prints alongside gifts of herbs or dried meat on my doorstep in the mornings. Sometimes she would venture inside and poke at my collection of drying plants and medical instruments. "Not anymore," I told her.

After my daughter's death I wasn't keen on being a healer, but my Coyote Girl wouldn't let me quit. She shyly offered me cut or broken fingers to tend, and reluctantly, I once again wielded herb and poultice. Her intensity drew me out of my sorrow enough to exchange what knowledge of healing I could without her speaking.

Now she was back, and I was frightened that she'd traveled so far in so poor a condition. "Come inside and into the light and tell me what's wrong." I gestured, and she followed me, hyperalert as if she expected to be ambushed.

Once indoors, she wordlessly pulled the neck of her shirt aside just far enough to show me the shrapnel studding her upper arm and the musket ball hole in her shoulder. I winced, remembering too many ailing soldiers in the camps. The wounds still bled sluggishly and her breathing was faster than it should have been. To my dismay, there was no matching injury on her back.

"It'll have to come out." I tried to keep my voice even since my nerves were getting the better of me at the thought of doing any kind of surgery. She gave a short, sharp nod, the only assent I would get, and sat on the edge of my cot.

I didn't have to ask how she'd been injured. I'd seen a detachment of Union Army infantry, including wagons, horses and two mountain howitzers, travel through the pass the Spaniards had called *Puerto del Dado*, the Pass of Chance. It separated the Chiricahua and Dos Cabezas mountains and housed a spring vital to those that lived in the area. The soldiers would have made for the water, and from the gunfire that began around noon and lasted for six grueling hours, the Apaches had done their best to prevent them from reaching it.

And now she was here, and likely not the only one of her people injured. I wasn't sure why she kept returning to me, since the Apaches knew perfectly well how to deal with bullet wounds. I was glad she did, though. She was brave and beautiful despite—or perhaps because of—her masculine clothing. And her ferocity and zest for life kindled a desire in me I'd felt for no other.

She smelled of dust and sweat and gunpowder, not surprising in this July heat, and I felt myself flush as I always did in her presence. "I have to tend to that wound. To do that, it, and you, have to be clean."

Her eyes narrowed. The clothes were her protection. Against what, I didn't know, and probably never would, and it didn't matter. She trusted me enough to remove them, and refused my assistance even when it was obvious her injury pained her. I let her be and set a kettle of water over the fire to heat. When I looked at her again, she'd gotten her shirt off and wore only her britches and the length of linen she'd wrapped around her chest to keep her breasts from being a hindrance. The linen, too, was soaked with blood and sweat. A leather belt wrapped around her slender hips, holding both her six-shooter and knife, and her rifle stood nearby within easy reach.

I gestured to the binding. "Take it off. We'll wash it." I had to admit to not being entirely altruistic with my request. There were so many layers to her, and while I'd never be able to know them all, I wanted to know, and touch, what I could. Bodies told stories as well, or sometimes better than, words.

She glared at me. She might have been eighteen or twenty-five, so difficult was her age to tell from the hard life she'd led. I loved her strength of expression. She was a fierce fighter with a body lean and hard and strong as any man's.

Yet when I carefully touched the binding, she relented. I unwrapped it to see scars, some old, some new, across her back and shoulders. Now she would have a few more.

She crossed her good arm over her bosom and sat, mute as always, while I took a damp cloth and wiped at her face and neck. There were no tears, not that I'd expected any, but I felt her anguish all the same. Her eyes followed me while the rest of her remained completely unresponsive to my careful ministrations. Tenderness was sometimes hard to accept during a time of war. There was so much urgency and worry and a never-ending tension that I felt in every muscle of her body, and I didn't know what, if anything, I could do to relieve it.

When I'd bathed as much of her as I could, she lay down, jaw set in preparation of what was to come. A table would have been better for surgeries, but all I had was my sturdy army cot, which would have to do. I lit every lantern and candle I had, set them nearby and laid out a bundle of clean rags. When it came to readying the knife, though, my hands began to shake. Panic surged in my belly. My daughter had died here, in that very bed. A thousand miles away, my husband had perished of gangrene and dysentery. I hadn't been able to save either of them, and I couldn't figure out why Coyote Girl trusted me to tend to her. Surely whatever gods had once watched over me had long since gone and taken my self-confidence with them.

A warm, calloused hand covered mine, and squeezed. I looked into her eyes and saw the faith I so sorely lacked. Gently, she moved my hand to the knife and held it until I was steady.

There was no help for it now. "I'm sorry," was all I said before I dug into the wound.

It's a brutal process under any circumstances. I'd learned from a Confederate Army doctor how to enlarge the wound just enough so I could get the forceps around the musket ball, but I hated the necessity of it and the damage I had to cause in order to remove any foreign objects. That done, I used tweezers to tease out the bits of shrapnel, painstaking because there were dozens of tiny metal fragments and I had to make certain to get them all.

She was pale and perspiring by the time I was done, but she hadn't made a sound. I cleaned the wounds, stitched the largest shut then had her sit up so I could dress and bind it. By then, her color had returned and I lent her my blanket to cover herself with while I cleaned up and put her laundry in the kettle to boil.

"Musket ball," I said, holding out a chunk of lead no doubt fired from one of the howitzers. "Want it for a souvenir?"

She reached for it, but instead of picking up the ball, she grasped my hand. Her fingers were rough and warm and strong enough to break my hand if she chose.

She met my gaze and held it. She'd never spoken to me. Other than our first meeting, I'd not heard her voice at all. Whether or not she spoke my languages, it didn't matter. I knew she understood, and she didn't need words to make her needs known at all. There was fear in her eyes, not of me, but of the terrible battle that afternoon. I doubted she'd ever seen a howitzer before, much less been on the receiving end of its fire. She'd seen things she did not understand, and sought comfort with someone who might.

"*Chica coyote,*" I said, and dared to caress her face. Her expression lost some of its hardness and she leaned into my touch, seeking the same comfort I craved. We'd both lost families and homes and the life we'd known. I'd had a husband, once, a white soldier who'd given me a home and a child before he'd gone to war and come home so badly wounded that none of my skills could save him. He'd done his duties as a husband, being serviceable in bed but no more, and I'd thought that was all there was to the art of love.

Until now, when Coyote Girl nuzzled the soft, ticklish spots between my neck and shoulders and sent delight shuddering all the way to my toes. One hand found my breast, squeezed, and pawed at my blouse until I pulled it down over my shoulders to reveal my chemise, which I hastily unbuttoned to leave my bosom as bare as hers.

Her fierce exterior hid a tender heart. This I found out as I pulled her to me and we were skin to skin, breasts against one another. It felt so perfect. So *right.*

I clutched at her, touching each scar, memorizing its place and wondering what might have caused it and what another healer had done to mend it. There was one along her spine, two on her good shoulder, one on her belly that vanished beneath her britches.

There was no softness to her; she was all strength and muscle as she pressed me onto the cot and held me there, nipping first at one nipple and then the other just lightly enough to tease instead of hurt. Darts of sensation prickled my body.

Then I noticed how much weight she was putting on her arms. "You be careful. You're injured!"

She didn't smile, not quite, but there was a hint of amusement in her eyes. It wasn't in her nature to take anything easy, even when I'd just spent an hour patching her up. My own husband had never been so eager. Nor had he thrust up my skirt, kneed my legs wide and put his hand...*there*.

A thrill of delight went through me as she stroked tender zones, fingers going in circles until I squirmed from the pleasurable ache. Wetness slicked my intimate places and she took advantage of this, rubbing faster and harder until I moaned from the throbbing tightness down below. Pressure and tension built, which left me nervous and a little afraid. I didn't know what would happen, only that it felt like my body would burst from her fierce attention.

Moments later, I arched upward as my body seized in a sort of contraction. A flush rolled through me. I closed my eyes, reveling in this new, enjoyable sensation and glad beyond measure it was my Coyote Girl who'd shown me. I would never know all her secrets, but this was a gift beyond price. She trusted me, *wanted* me, and in turn revealed to me wonders I'd never guessed at. Although he'd never purposely hurt me, my husband had never bothered with my enjoyment. The prostitutes who'd come to me for medicine never spoke of such delights.

So as the throbbing eased, leaving me languid and worn, I was rendered as speechless as my guest.

Oh, my trickster girl. I loved her even more for the satisfied, calculating expression she now wore.

She wasn't done, either. I watched with eager anticipation as she stood just long enough to undo her belt and, careful of her gun and knife, step out of her britches and knee-high moccasins. The sight of her astounded me, all edge and sharpness instead of the soft, rounded women I'd grown up with. Wasting no time, she clambered back onto the cot and straddled my hips.

Having aided in dozens of births, I was no stranger to the female body, but it was a wonder to touch it for the sole purpose of bringing pleasure. My fingers slipped easily into her folds, and with her hand atop mine, I pressed harder and deeper as she urged me on. My own body tingled in response as I scented her, explored her, tucked a finger inside her and shuddered at the feel of that soft, moist interior.

Head back, eyes closed, she rode me, hips rocking, her hand firmly keeping mine in place. I listened to the harsh sounds of her breath, the wetness of her moving against my hand. She gave a little gasp, tensed and shuddered just as her body began an intense, rhythmic squeezing.

With my free hand, I sought the slickness of my own body and rubbed frantically, desperate to feel that same bodily urgency once more. Coyote Girl, probably amused by my immodesty, eased aside and added a hand to mine. One finger slipped inside me. Two. I arched back, wanting to feel more of her, and she obliged, driving into me as deeply as she could.

The tide within me surged, rose, and with one last thrust, toppled me over the edge. My body squeezed around her fingers as if desperate to keep them there forever. Tingling jolts shot through my legs, all the way down to my toes, which spasmed from the excitement of it all.

I let out a howl, and for the first time—she laughed. The sound stunned me into silence, and after a moment, she too let out a yip that would have done a coyote proud.

I joined in, feeling childish and silly yet somehow free. It was just the two of us, and for a few brief moments, the rest of the world vanished. We were two crazy women out in the wilderness leading wildly different lives, but ever so briefly the spirits had blessed our joining and made us something more.

When we'd howled ourselves hoarse, we toppled into the cot, snugged tight against each other, and simply lay there, too tired to move.

After a while, she relaxed into sleep, but our exertions had left me too flushed to do the same. I carefully extricated myself and, wearing only my chemise, I scrubbed her clothes clean. I glanced at her every now and then. She was curled up, resting on her uninjured side. There was no blood on the bandages, thank goodness, despite our exercise. For the rest of the night, I watched the firelight flicker across her bare skin, memorizing every inch of her in preparation for the moment I would have to let her go.

It wasn't yet dawn when she woke. I passed her clothes to her. They were still damp although I'd dried them as best I could. She didn't seem to care, and let me help her with the binding so as not to stress her injured shoulder.

"Stay here," I begged, although I knew it was in vain. Duty and love for her people overrode anything I might ask of her, and I admired her all the more for her determination.

She pulled me close, pressing her forehead to mine. We stayed like that for a few heartbeats, breathing in each other's scents, savoring the moment.

Then, abruptly, she released me, grabbed her rifle and headed to the door. Stunned and heartbroken I watched her go, terrified I would lose her, too.

I dashed after her. The faintest hints of dawn were just beginning to light the sky, and I could not see her. She'd disappeared as she always had, blending into the shadows and silent as her namesake.

Later, as the sun rose, the sounds of artillery echoing off the hills broke the peace of the morning. I rushed outside, wrapped my shawl around my shoulders and stepped onto the porch. I prayed for my Coyote Girl and everyone else caught in the battle. I'd seen enough deaths, and this land needed no more.

At dusk, I waited for her, hoping beyond hope she would return. There was no sign of her. In the morning, a string of cavalry passed nearby. The soldiers spoke of how they'd secured the spring, and there was talk of building a fort in the area so they could retain control of the land. My heart sank. Coyote Girl and her people had lost, then. She wouldn't be coming back. There was no longer any reason for me to stay.

With a heavy heart I spent the day packing medicines and

tools and tidying my little hut for the last time. The next morning dawned warm and clear. A fine day to continue my journey, to embrace life rather than hide from it.

And there, not more than a few steps from my door, a musket ball lay in a circle of coyote prints. I picked it up, felt the weight and warmth of it as I rolled it around in my hand, and smiled. I could not have been left a clearer message.

I headed down the trail, steady of heart and hand and filled with a newfound sense of purpose. My coyote girl would never give up the fight, and neither would I.

SPA DAY

Taylor C. Dunne

Summer came early to Washington, DC, leaving the air sticky and heavy as lead by late April. The lobby of the Chesapeake Hotel and Spa, however, was cool and sleek, all heavy marble with chrome accents, incongruous in the throng of staid government-issued architecture. Even all that marble couldn't keep the humidity from seeping in under the doors, though. Walking outside, Catherine thought, felt like walking into a mouth—she ran a hand self-consciously over her sleek dark hair as she quickened her pace to make the last few strides through the door. She could feel the strands at the nape of her neck already frizzing from the heat.

It was Georgia's idea that they should get away for a while, and so Catherine was ready to bestow the credit upon her for the restorative nature of this trip. She'd booked a suite at the Chesapeake—their usual—and whisked Catherine away to Annapolis early in the morning, citing her tense shoulders, her stiff posture. "I've never seen anyone more in need of a deep tissue massage," Georgia said knowingly. "And a facial. Your skin looks parched, baby, have you been moisturizing?"

Catherine lifted the back of her hand to her cheek and stroked it absentmindedly. "Not as often as I should," she admitted. "It's just—we've been so busy at work. Half the time I get home and barely have the energy to take off my makeup."

Georgia clicked her tongue, disapproving. When they arrived at the spa, she ordered for Catherine—the botanical facial, the red-flower body massage, a sugar waxing, a quick trim-up on her haircut. Catherine didn't question it, just tacked on a request for a pedicure. No manicure. Keeping her nails plain, blunt and short, was her mildest form of rebellion against the guise demanded of her in public.

It turned out to be exactly what she needed, truth be told, the stress of the workweek melting away under the capable hands of the masseuse. They spent the rest of the day together, sipping sparkling wine and nibbling strawberries, the conversation light and cozy, not quite required. The staff, as usual, deferred to Georgia's authority; they seemed to pay the specificities of their relationship to each other no regard. After all, to much of the country, Georgia was merely one of the most powerful women in finance; her close relationship with her executive assistant raised few eyebrows save for in their innermost circles. By the end of the day, when they retired to their suite upstairs, Catherine felt altogether more relaxed than she had in weeks.

They lounged in the room for a while, losing track of time. Catherine fixed them both a drink from the minibar, and between the makeshift screwdrivers she shook up with pineapple juice instead of orange, and the rosé they'd been sipping all day, she soon found herself loose and comfortable in her own skin, wrapped in a plush white bathrobe. She sprawled comfortably by the window, the Chesapeake Bay glittering in the background as she listened to Georgia crisply tapping the keyboard of her laptop.

Some interminable amount of time passed before Georgia turned her attention to Catherine, who was seated on the fainting couch by the window, paging through a copy of the *Atlantic* and idly twisting a strand of fresh-cut hair along one finger. Georgia bent down by her side, tipped her chin up and drew her into a warm kiss. Catherine sighed into it, the buildup of the day bubbling to the surface. Georgia kissed like a dream, soft and smooth but bossy enough to make her shiver a little, to remind her where she belonged. Where she *liked* to belong.

Georgia patted the California king bed. "Sit," she said, and Catherine sat obediently, stretching out along the mattress, letting her robe fall temptingly askew. She watched Georgia from the corner of one eye, as she rifled through her suitcase, clearly looking for something in particular. She sat it on the bed, and Catherine cocked a brow—

"You certainly came prepared," Catherine laughed, and Georgia hummed in agreement as she shed her own robe. Her body still often caught Catherine by surprise, alternating firm and soft and supple and well built in harmony, and her dark-brown skin glowed from the massage. It was altogether too much, and Catherine's breath caught in her throat as she stretched out farther, arranging herself on the pillow and beckoning for Georgia to kneel over her face.

She always worked best with one task to focus on, one singular activity upon which to center all of her energy and abilities. This, then, remained her favorite iteration of that particular quirk of personality. She slid her pale hands up along Georgia's thighs, grasping them from the outside as she lifted her head just enough off the pillow to angle it right against Georgia's cunt. She ran her tongue along her outer lips, featherlight touches that grew a little more firm each time.

When she touched her tongue to Georgia's clit, she earned a hand in the hair and a warm "Good girl," and she flushed. *Yes, very good*, she thought. She relaxed into a rhythm, long broad strokes with the flat of her tongue followed by smaller flicks, and when she had Georgia panting above her, grasping at her hair with a firmer hand, her eyes fluttered up to look her in the face as she closed her mouth over Georgia's clit and sucked.

"Oh, good girl," Georgia groaned again, hips bucking against her face. "Stay right like that, don't stop—" and it was just on the right side of overwhelming, to be so willingly caged by Georgia's long legs and her firm thighs; Catherine dug fingers into her hips and held her there, breathing raggedly through her nose as she drew what felt like an endless orgasm from her. It was everything, and Catherine was nothing but the weight of her lover's body and the salty heat of her cunt upon her lips.

She licked her swollen lips as Georgia daintily lifted herself away, and caught Georgia smiling cagily in response. "Thank you," Catherine said, perhaps unnecessarily under the circumstances. But she meant it. Georgia kissed her on the lips as she sat up and licked into her mouth, hot and dirty, and Catherine realized, suddenly, how wet she was herself. She hastily undid the tie on the bathrobe and tossed it away, shaking her dark, glossy bob out of her face with satisfaction.

Georgia stood up from the bed and stepped carefully into the harness. "How long has it been since I've fucked your ass?" she asked, warm and casual, and Catherine felt her entire face flush down to her collarbone, her body growing warm.

"Ah," she said, at a loss for words. "I suppose—since the G20 in Paris."

Georgia chuckled as she secured their cock in the harness. It was the glass one, heavy and exquisitely crafted, and she ran one hand along it suggestively as she tightened the straps. "Would you like me to do that tonight?" she asked, voice low and teasing, and Catherine swallowed, nodding shakily. Her cunt answered for her in the affirmative, as she felt a throb of arousal pulse through her at the way Georgia stroked the glass shaft expectantly, waiting.

Catherine forced out an answer. "Yes, Ma'am," she muttered,

eyes lowered, and Georgia grinned and bent to kiss her once more before patting her firmly on the hip.

"Turn over," she said decisively, and Catherine obeyed, arranging herself on all fours. Her hair fell back into her eyes as she rested her head delicately on a pillow, and she felt Georgia brush it out of the way, stroking her cheek with affection. "You look so beautiful, love," she murmured, "so willing and trusting. Gonna make this so good for you."

"You always do," Catherine said in half a whisper, and Georgia smiled before moving back to the center of the bed.

"Up," Georgia ordered decisively, smacking her once on the ass, and Catherine arched her back, displaying herself properly. "So pretty, baby. Why don't you spread yourself for me? Show me what I'm working with?"

Catherine's entire body went hot and buzzing at that, but on instinct, she pushed her face harder against the pillow as she reached back to obey, displaying herself. She felt a rivulet of arousal trickling down her thigh as she did. *Fuck.*

Georgia's hand slid along the underside of her stomach, thumb brushing at her clit, the barest hint of pressure. One finger stroked up through the wet heat of her center, fingertip just dipping inside, and Catherine resisted the urge to rock back on it. But only barely. She was already nearly shaking with the effort of holding back, of staying perfectly still.

Georgia took her hand away, and Catherine glanced back over her shoulder to see her sucking it into her mouth, humming around it. "You taste so good, my love," she murmured. There was another throb of heat, another pulse of arousal, and Catherine spread herself a little wider, arched her back a little farther, silently begging with wide, cloudy eyes.

"Good girl," Georgia said, "stay just like that," and then she dipped her head to lick a stripe up from her cunt to the cleft of her ass, followed by another, and another. Catherine's hips bucked on instinct. Her body shook with the effort of not moving more openly as Georgia rubbed at her clit with the heel of her palm. Lightly, at first, and then more insistently, giving her something solid to grind against as Georgia continued to eat her out. And then there was a finger tracing the rim of her entrance, slick with lube and her own juices, and she whimpered as she arched her back a little more, relaxed every muscle, let Georgia press inside her while still working her clit with her other hand. She wanted to pretend it hadn't been a while, that the sensation wasn't new all over again, but the initial burn quickly relaxed into an intense feeling of fullness that she always forgot she loved—

It was almost too good. Catherine gasped and babbled into the pillow as she let the sensation overwhelm her, as another finger joined the first, working her loose and open—allowing Georgia to draw out one quick orgasm that hit her as fast and sharp as a smack to the face.

Her chest heaved as she rode it over the edge and came back to earth. All she could think was *more*—an insatiable need rose within her, a desire to be filled in a most unladylike way, used until she was panting and screaming and limp. An interminable moment passed, and she looked back to see Georgia slicking up the thick glass cock, hand moving up and down with a strange sort of grace.

"What do you want, Catherine?" she asked, her voice low and smooth and warm, thumb brushing over the head of the strap-on. "Go ahead. Tell me what you want."

Catherine clenched her jaw; she swallowed hard, her cunt throbbing hot and tight. "I want you to fuck me," she muttered, a half answer, half into the pillow. She shut her eyes, felt the head of the dildo rubbing along her cleft, dug her fingertips into where she still obediently held herself open. (She thought, briefly, about letting go. *I didn't tell you to stop*, she could hear Georgia chiding already; she clenched her fingers a little tighter.)

"Is that all?" Georgia asked, and the cock rubbed back and

forth, back and forth, heavy and thick and not enough, and Catherine swallowed again.

"Please, Ma'am," she mumbled through taut humiliation. "I—I want you to fuck my ass."

"Good girl," Georgia said, effusive and sweet and encouraging, and she took half a moment of anticipation before she positioned the head at Catherine's entrance and slowly, excruciatingly slowly, pressed inside.

Catherine closed her eyes and let out a long breath. The sensation was intense and just this side of too much—Georgia took it so slowly, filling her up a quarter inch at a time, a long, unbroken thrust until she was fully seated inside Catherine, the leather straps of the harness flush against her ass. And then she felt Georgia take hold of her hands, moving them down to the mattress. "You should hold on," she said quietly. "Good girl. Hold on for me." Catherine swallowed and gripped the sheets with both hands, spreading her legs wider and shifting her weight on her knees. "I want you to come again," Georgia added, warm but authoritative; it was no idle desire. "Play with your cunt if you have to."

Catherine didn't need to be told twice. She rubbed her clit in small circles, soft where she still felt overstimulated and then harder as Georgia began to fuck her in slow, small, but steady strokes. Her face was burning warm and damp with sweat. Her hair stuck to her forehead as she shifted position on the pillow— more, more, more, her body screamed, and as Georgia paused, a silent check-in, she clenched her jaw and pushed back harder onto the cock inside her.

"Oh, you like that, don't you?" Georgia said with a fond laugh, matching Catherine's thrust with one of her own. "My dirty girl. That's okay. I've got you." She took her hips in both hands, then, and began to fuck her in earnest, long, rolling thrusts, hitting nerve endings she didn't even know she possessed—and she was begging, she knew she was begging, a cascade of *pleases* and *thank-yous* pouring from her parted lips as Georgia fucked her—

Her second orgasm started deep in her core, all of her nerves vibrating at once, singing, shredded, dissolving. She buried her face in the pillow, holding on with one hand, Georgia fucking her through it as she let out a ragged, wordless shriek only barely muffled by the goose down as she collapsed, prone, onto it.

She sensed time slowing down, somehow; felt Georgia pulling out of her, felt the rustle of movement and a sudden sensation of emptiness and seconds that could be minutes or vice versa, really, she wouldn't know. She didn't come back to earth until she felt Georgia turning her onto her side, pulling her close. The harness was gone, nothing between them but skin on skin, and then a blanket resting lightly over the top as she shivered. She was hot, but the sweat coating her body gave her chills, and Georgia ran smooth hands over her skin reverently, kissing her neck and shoulders, kissing the tension out.

Georgia was soaking wet. Catherine felt it as she slid one leg in between the two of hers. She was not so far gone, she thought, and reached down to work Georgia through a slow, easy orgasm, two fingers inside and thumb rubbing against her languid and easy. They were both a sticky mess as they collapsed into each other, the spa's painstaking handiwork practically destroyed.

"We should think about dinner soon," Georgia said after a brief pause, dropping another row of affectionate kisses along the line of Catherine's shoulder. "Perhaps just room service."

Catherine half shrugged in response, considering the notion. "Whatever you'd like," she said truthfully. "I trust your judgment."

REVENANT

Vanessa de Sade

It had been over twenty-five years since Trudy had last seen Fiona, and she stands hesitantly now on the immaculately scrubbed doorstep, not quite sure if she should press the bell or just run away. The two of them had been as thick as thieves back in their art school days, of course, sharing a studio and gleefully getting themselves covered in gouache on a regular basis, frenzied young painters hell-bent on becoming the next Jenny Saville. But that was before Fiona had gone and met some dickhead bloke and ditched college to marry him; and Trudy herself had taken a U-turn and changed her art degree to one in Renaissance history. And yet here she is today, trim and successful in her immaculate Calvin Klein suit, inhaling the scent of polish and trying to still her beating heart.

They had drifted apart after Fiona had married. Jack, the new husband, was disapproving of Trudy and Fiona's other arty friends; and though the pair still exchanged Christmas cards— Trudy's expensive gallery reproductions of Renaissance masterpieces; Fiona's bland supermarket representations of robins and pinecones—they had not spoken in over two decades. And yet, here Trudy is like the proverbial bad penny, deep in the heart of suburbia, surveying the neatly mown lawn and regulation flowerbed with two stultified rosebushes not quite daring to bloom, milk bottles carefully rinsed and stacked in a little metal container on the step, an old-style coir doormat hesitatingly bearing the word WELCOME, and everything polished to within an inch of its life and gleaming like a new pin.

Oh, what the fuck! Trudy swallows and rings the bell. She can hear it chiming somewhere deep in the bowels of the house. *Ding-dong.* Avon calling. Hell, this is a *really* stupid idea. Fiona probably won't even know her. Probably isn't in. *This is a fool's errand!* Yet she hears the unmistakable sound of slippered feet and a shadow passes over the sunburst window in the paneled front door, the paint blistering just a bit, but still a definite shade of old-fashioned baize green.

And the scent of polish is so much stronger as the door opens. Lavender polish. The kind your mother used to buy from the Betterware man. "Yes?" It's a woman's voice. Brisk. Defensive. *Who the fuck are you* implied in its tone.

"Hello, Fiona…"

She's blinking uncertainly in the bright light of the after-noon sun. The hair that used to be an untamed tangle of unruly blonde tresses now cut short and showing some traces of gray. Salt and pepper her mother would call it. Wearing an expensive but shapeless slubby dress and a precisely pressed floral apron. Tan tights. Tartan slippers on her feet. In the background Trudy can hear a radio and the closing music to "The Archers," the tweet of a canary in a cage. There is cabbage-rose paper on the wall and a collection of Goldscheider plaster masks tapering back into the gloom.

"Trudy? Holy fuck, *Trudy?* Is that really you?"

They look at each other for a long moment, staring in disbe-lief at what they've become, and then suddenly they're in each other's arms, embracing, the years melting away, and they're just two young hopefuls taking on the world once again.

"Trudy, Trudy, look at you in your power suit and heels. What happened to you?"

Trudy laughs. Points. "Look at yourself, Mrs. Home Counties, when did *you* go and get all twinset and pearls? Not to mention this house. It's like something out of a museum…"

Now it's Fiona's turn to laugh, putting her arm around her friend and leading her inside. "It *is* a museum. The museum of Mabel, my dearly departed mother-in-law. We inherited this place when the old girl kicked the bucket and Jack insisted that we keep it just the way she left it. Wait till you see the living room!"

"And you've lived here like this, all these years? What happened to your dreams? Your painting?"

"Ah, I could ask you the same question, Mrs. Chair of Renaissance Art. What happened to *your* dreams? And your painting, for that matter. What happened to that?"

Trudy looks sheepish. "Seems that talking about dead painters pays a lot more than creating your own art," she admits. "That's the world we live in…"

They're both in the lounge by now, leatherette suite and a low-slung coffee table with spindly brass-tipped legs and a kitsch painting of flamingos on its glazed upper surface. Scores of pictures of Jack as a boy lining the top of an upright piano that doesn't look as if it's been played in decades. Wallpaper in a chintz pattern, faded where the afternoon sun slants in through the big bay window.

Fiona sighs. "What a pair of turncoats we turned out to be. But why are you here, Trudy? Not that I'm not delighted to see you, of course, but why now after all this time?"

Trudy shrugs. "I was on the way somewhere from someplace else and I suddenly thought of you. My flight's not until tomorrow and I thought, well, why not. So, here I am. I thought we could maybe spend some time together, you know, catch up…"

"Catch up?"

"Yes, you know, talk about old times. Reminisce."

"Reminisce?" Fiona's eyes are suddenly blazing. "I don't want to fucking reminisce."

Trudy meets her gaze. Defiant. "Then what?"

"You know what."

"Seriously? Now?"

Fiona nods, her big breasts rising and falling, her voice breathless.

"Oh holy fuck…"

"Holy fuck is right," Fiona says in a low voice, a deep and bestial voice that comes from some other Fiona, some other life. Reaching for Trudy, pulling her close.

And their embrace is sudden but sweet. Their kiss hard and penetrating as they melt into each other's arms, tongues already inquisitive, the electric current between them palpable and crackling in the afternoon air like something out of an old monster movie, their two hearts hammering as they eat each other up.

"You always said no. Before, when I asked you, you always said no…" Trudy protests as she comes up for air.

"I was nineteen and wanted to have babies, you idiot, of course I said no. It doesn't mean I meant it…"

They kiss again. Desperately. Hot and horny for each other. Trudy smells of some expensive perfume that comes packed in a sculptural bottle and costs the earth. Fiona's aroma is simple own-brand apple shampoo and more powerful than any pheromone. And Trudy wants to gobble her up like a homemade cherry pie, all soft and sugary pastry on the outside with a thick sticky sauce beneath that oozes onto the plate and has to be licked.

"Come on, upstairs. He doesn't get home till after seven on a Thursday. We've plenty of time…"

"I didn't come here to do this…"

"Like fuck you didn't. You're as ravenous as I am!"

They're in the bedroom by now. A slightly musty smell of old wardrobes and camphor. Same cabbage-rose paper as the downstairs hall. The light low, like an old cinema before the matinee. Velvet drapes drawn in daylight to save the carpet. A neat dressing table with an unused silver brush and mirror set, a double bed with a green satin coverlet. Embroidered with a simple central flower. A homemade rag rug, incongruous on the thickly carpeted floor. Trudy recognizes the style. This is Fiona's one attempt to assert herself in this silent temple to a dead woman's taste.

And in the slight chill of someone else's domain Trudy feels suddenly dwarfed, and so Fiona takes charge. Kisses her again. On the lips then down the whole length of her long white swan's neck. Turning Trudy's knees to water. Oh yes, this is what she came here for, *yes indeedy,* but she had never even dared to hope.

"Do you have anyone? Can I mark you?"

"No, no-one. And yes, yes please, do it all you want…"

She feels Fiona's lips sucking hard on the fleshy nape of her neck, then her teeth sink in and she wants to weep with pleasure. She's due to give a lecture on the metaphysical imagery in Leonardo da Vinci's *The Last Supper* in Copenhagen two days from now and will have to find a suitable scarf to cover the huge red blemish on her throat, or maybe not. Fuck it, let them all conjecture. Out loud, she groans: "Naked, I want you naked!"

Fiona grins and pushes her down onto the bed. "You've seen me naked before, what's the big deal?"

"Stop teasing and get your kit off before I rip that awful dress down the middle and rape you."

"Promises, promises. Here, unzip me…"

She slides out of the slubby green sheath like a serpent shedding its skin and transforms into a symphony in creams and whites, her body an arctic landscape of untouched snow, Leda and the Swan, Venus ascending, rounded and pleasing despite the unflattering white bra that fails miserably to contain her big, full breasts. Hipster panties in ivory cotton beneath the tights, her belly rounded, pudenda huge and pronounced under the knickers, hint of a tantalizing camel toe nestled at the crotch.

"You still like?" she asks, kneeling over Trudy's recumbent form, straddling her like a colossus. "Still as desperate to fuck me now that I'm a fat old woman?"

Trudy nods, breathless. *Oh fuck yeah!* Pulls the waistband of the tights and panties out with one trembling hand, slides the other deep inside. Feels smooth skin like silk, thick fur, slippery wetness. "Take your bra off."

Fiona tries to smile but she's panting by now and her clit is as hard as a lubricious pecan. And her hand shakes as she reaches for the catch on her own brassiere, her huge tits tumbling out like a snowy avalanche, the nipples up like ramrods, unexpectedly dark garnet red in color, not sugar pink like most of the blondes Trudy has fucked. Then Fiona yanks her own pants down to her knees, ripping her panty hose, and flops down on top of Trudy, the two of them kissing like their lives depend on it.

"Have you done this before?" Trudy asks, pulling Fiona's panties right off and feasting her eyes on her friend's cunt, the thick white-blonde hair so fine it's as if she's shaved, her pouty pussy lips begging to be kissed.

"Yes. With my best friend when I was fourteen."

"Shit, everyone does it with their best friend when they're fourteen. I mean have you ever done this *properly*, with another grown-up woman?"

Fiona closes her eyes for a moment, luxuriating in what Trudy's fingers are doing to her cunt, slowly pulling it open like a split fig and circling that big throbbing clit. Treating it to the occasional flick that drives her wild. "No," she whispers. "You're my first." Though this isn't strictly true.

Because there was that day when she found the box of

magazines under the bed in her sons' room, and she'd pored over page after garishly colored page of splayed women, black and white, fat and skinny, hairy and shaved, big tits, little tits, a cornucopia of female pulchritude, and she'd touched herself. Yes, touched herself right there, rubbed herself, massaged her big fat clit until the orgasm ripped itself out of her and made her scream with pent-up rage. Sneaking up to the boys' room every afternoon to do it again. Bereft when they both fucked off to university without a backward glance and took their wank-stack with them, leaving her alone with the knowledge of *exactly* what she was.

And now Trudy was back in her life for one magical after-noon. Insistent little Trudy who had always been so desperate to experiment in their tiny attic studio, with each of them taking turns to pose nude while the other drew, Trudy's furry little pussy with its tight and secret slit like a perfect keyhole so delicious and appealing. But Fiona had wanted babies and a husband who would provide, hadn't wanted to bump cunts with another girl now that they were grown up and responsible adults. *That wasn't how it was done,* she had told herself. Had even believed it for a while.

"You've had girls though?" she asks now, maybe accuses, tugging impatiently at the buttons on Trudy's white silk blouse, the suit jacket lost somewhere between the lounge and here. "You've fucked other women, I know you have!"

"I have, but I've always hungered for what I couldn't get," Trudy pants, ripping off her shirt and wriggling out of her skirt. She has on a tiny Westwood thong in deep pomegranate and black with a matching bra cupping her small breasts, and soft chestnut curls peep deliciously from the hinge of her thighs. "Sooner or later, I'd end up imagining that they were you."

Fiona pulls the silken ribbon on Trudy's hip and gasps as her panties unfurl, Trudy's bush like a soft puffball, a catkin, a sexy bunny tail at the gateway to enchantment. "I always think about you when Jack fucks me," she confesses. "I visualize sucking your tits when I want to come."

"Suck away then," Trudy groans, pulling off her bra and baring her little nubs, the perky brown nipples erect and rubbery. Areolas huge, like old half crowns.

"God, I want to eat you," Fiona gasps. "Will you show me how?"

Trudy laughs though the breath is rasping out of her like an exhausted long-distance runner's. "Do to me what I do to you," she manages to gasp, shivering as Fiona's fingers stroke her tits and pinch the nipples.

"I've never touched another woman's pussy before," Fiona admits, one hand circling Trudy's chubby little pudenda. "We just touched tits when we were kids…"

"You'll love it, and touching yours is pure heaven," Trudy kisses back into her ear, her breath hot. "Just pet me gently like this, that's right, just stroke the hair to begin with, now press a little harder, yes, just like that, now push inside, I'm so wet that you'll slide right in…"

"You're so slippery, and so hot. Oh god, Trudy, I think I'm going to come!"

"Me too, rub me hard!"

And they could both feel it, feel the throbbing ache within themselves like a piece of machinery being wound past its limit and about to snap, a river in spate beating at its banks, a dam about to burst, and then suddenly they are kissing and scratching and screaming and bucking like unbroken mares, their fingers deep in each other's slit, humping furiously against each other, their fervent kisses sharing each other's orgasm as wave after wave engulfs them.

"And *now* you're going to get eaten," Trudy manages to whisper, as she flips herself around and bends her head to Fiona's fat and furry cunt. "Now I'm going to show you what a real orgasm feels like!"

"I never came like that in twenty-five years of marriage," Fiona's voice filters down as she rubs her face against Trudy's bush. "It can't get any better. Can it?"

"Wait till you taste me," Trudy promises, her own tongue starting to map all of Fiona's secret pink lips like a cartographer measuring contours. "Believe me, once you've eaten pussy nothing else will ever compare. Oh, holy fuck, Fiona, I've waited all my life to do this…"

"Me too," Fiona agrees, kissing, kissing, a sugar baby oozing sweetness, not daring to lick quite yet, just breathing in all Trudy's scents, pheromones, hungering for her taste. Her honeyed nectar. "Do it really slow," she breathes. "I want this to last forever…"

They make love all afternoon and dangerously late into the pink-streaked sky of early evening, and it won't be long before Jack's sedate little car pulls into the drive, his key slides into the worn brass lock on the old green-baize door downstairs. Does he shout, *Honey, I'm home,* Trudy wonders as she gathers her clothes from where they have been strewn all over the bedroom floor, her hair still damp form the shower where Fiona slid into the cubicle and went down on her as she shampooed. It has been heaven on earth, a fairy-tale romance, but like all good fairy tales the princesses must make themselves scarce before the giant awakens, or suffer the consequences in the land beyond the beanstalk.

"I don't want to go," Trudy whispers, holding Fiona tight, traitorous tears betraying how much the ice maiden really feels inside.

"You have to go," says the ever-practical Fiona. Coldly, Trudy thinks. "You have a job. Commitments."

"Fuck my commitments. It's you I want."

"You mean that?"

"With all my heart."

"Then..."

"Then?"

"Then there is a way. I have a little money put by and Jack's Range Rover is in the garage. I paid for it, and I'm an excellent driver. We could buy a caravan. I'll have you in Copenhagen in time for your lecture if we go now, catch the last ferry from Folkestone tonight."

"But your home? Your children?"

"Another woman's home, and my children don't know I exist. Jack saw to that..."

"Your marriage was...*terrible?*"

"Yes it was, but there's no time for all that boo-hoo stuff right now. Yes or no, Trudy?"

Trudy pauses. Doesn't hesitate. *Pauses.* She always was one for dramatic effect, the cow. "What do you think?" she grins. "Pack your stuff!"

But Fiona just picks up the keys to the Rover and puts her passport in her bag. "I don't need any stuff, and I don't want any of it, I'm starting a new life." Kisses Trudy. "With you."

"With me," Trudy grins, beaming like an adolescent being asked to her first prom. *"You're starting a new life with me!"*

And they kiss again, right there in the driveway for all the neighbors to see, before backing the Range Rover carefully onto the street and then speeding away toward the darkening eastern sky. And Fiona knows it won't be easy and they'll both have to give and take, have to learn each other's habits all over again; but they've lived together before and she knows that they can do it again. And, of course, there's so much beautiful sex they've yet to experience, so much love to make. And a caravan is a dull structure that won't take much looking after, maybe she could decorate it, stencil a pattern around the window frames or perhaps even design a mural for the interior walls. Maybe even start painting again...

OFF SEASON

Valerie Alexander

Shea had her admirers. Soccer fans and students screaming in the stands; straight girls bringing her brownies for the bus trips to games; ex-conquests grudgingly conceding she was a legendary goalie, even if she was a heartless slut off the field. And players from other Division I schools like me, who studied the team's game tapes even before I knew I was transferring to that university and it would be my team too. She was a thing of butch magnificence under the lights, a brooding jock of a girl with heroic shoulders and a stoic face that never changed as she guarded her goal.

I didn't talk to her at our first practice. Coach introduced me as the new center fullback and while some girls smiled and other girls said welcome, Shea's handsome face stayed impassive. She was squinting in the late afternoon sun, waiting for Coach to finish her opening season first practice pep talk so we could get on to the business of drills.

I tried not to look at her too much.

"Everyone gets along, no one's competitive in a mean way," said our sweeper Bridget when we went out for beef pho and pork rolls after practice. "Last year sucked because of Shea and Lana but then Lana transferred so—" She drank her water. "And now we have you."

Lana was the stopper I'd replaced. I'd studied her the most on the game tapes, her long coppery braid swinging as she booted the ball with powerful kicks. "They were...?"

"Oh, yeah. They thought no one knew, but we all knew. And then Shea slept with Lana's roommate and every practice, every game, was shit after that. Thank god Lana left before she ruined this season too."

"Seems like Shea ruined last season," I said.

"Eh," Bridget said. "Everyone knows what she's like. Who's stupid enough to fuck their teammate?"

Walking back to my apartment—not a dorm room, but a student housing apartment for athletes—I wondered how it felt for Shea to see me in front of her on the field, a shorter, curvier stranger with a honey-colored ponytail, instead of rail-thin Lana. During my penalty kick in practice, she'd watched me like I was any opponent trying to invade her goal, bent slightly with her floppy sun-bleached hair pushed back. She'd leapt up and caught my ball like a cat capturing a lame sparrow and released it back to us with a simple rise of her foot.

Soccer practice had always meant a few things to me: the hard crack of cleat kicking ball; the robin's-egg blue of the sky and the smell of grass; sweat trickling down my shirt and the hard breathing of girls around me while a coach lectured or cajoled or guided us. Walking home in autumn twilight with sore calves and blood still flowing with adrenalin. It didn't mean stealing glances across the field. Team romances were for summer leagues, not Division I athletes with their eyes on NCAA tournaments.

Shea, Bridget and four other stars were seniors, which made the season an emotional one for the school. Even our practices had their spectators, students lingering on the sidelines for the thrill of watching our sprints and drills and the occasional scrimmage. Shea and Hanna, our striker with cover-girl looks, had the most groupies, and most of us had at least one. I ignored mine: a shy boy who limited himself to one nervous wave per practice and a busty junior who was notorious for seducing female athletes.

"Stay away from her," Shea said to me one evening after practice. "She's a nutter."

"How do you know?"

"Because when I lived on campus, she talked my roommate into letting her wait naked in my room for me one night. Rose petals on the bed spelling out my jersey number."

"Did you call security?"

She gave me a weird look. "Why would I?" She headed over to Hanna, who was wrapping up her knee in a different part of the locker room.

It was our first conversation and I'd ruined it. I'd failed to grasp that dominant butch goalies lived a life of groupies and stalkers, that calling security was uncool. I always showered at home after practice but today I went into the sauna and let the heat and silence exorcise my thudding, tumultuous heart. A midfielder came in and stretched out on a bench; someone else left; I closed my eyes and tuned them out. When I opened my eyes, I was alone except for Shea sitting on the opposite redwood bench. She was naked with a white towel over her lap, arms stretched out to the side to show off her massive shoulders, her small muscular tits as hard and defined as pectorals. Her closed eyes relaxed her face's usual surly indifference and made her look almost noble.

She opened her eyes and we gazed at each other. She pulled off her towel and mopped her head with it, thighs open just enough to show me all of her pussy. Naked, she walked out of the sauna. I pushed my hand between my legs and brought myself off, quickly, desperately, ashamed at how fast I came for so little a show.

* * *

We played an old rival the following week, and their midfielder butted Hanna in the face in the first half, breaking her nose. We won 1-0 but it was a silent bus ride home, like everyone sensed that this season wasn't going to be the cakewalk of triumph everyone needed it to be. And then Coach announced we were playing in a special October tournament. Our opponent: the same college where Lana—our ex-teammate, Shea's scorned ex and scorched earth—had transferred.

"Good," Bridget said to me, wrapping up her chest before practice that week. "Lana will lose her shit all over again when she sees Shea. Advantage ours."

"It's been a year. She's probably over it."

"Not that psycho."

Nothing for me to think about. Not how it had happened between them, how it had gotten started; an aimless conversation during practice, maybe, when the front line was getting lectured down at the other goal. Lana noticing Shea's relentless focus on the ball, like a predator stalking its kill, or her primitive grunts when she sent the ball flying back to Hanna with one clean rebuff. Or maybe Shea just texted her one night, blunt and lazy: *Come over.* And then besotted Lana had probably been giving Shea her all until that wasn't enough and Shea callously fucked her roommate too.

So many ways it could have happened. Slipping into the woods behind campus, fucking up against the oak trees, or fingering each other in the equipment room. Trying not to exchange any meaningful looks during practice, the way I tried not to look at Shea now.

She barely acknowledged me. She backed me up like any good goalie, shouting encouragement when I was fighting in my full stopper glory, but she never looked at me when we were sprawled on the grass getting scolded by Coach. The sauna episode had been her showing off her lioness glory like she'd show anyone: *Behold my magnificence*, pulling away the towel had said. At Bridget's birthday party, Shea stayed on the couch all night with her fan club of flustered, adoring girls, one of whom gradually wound up on her lap. Shea idly played with her thighs under her dress, barely grunting answers as the other girls tried to impress her. I was nothing to her. But the pit in my stomach before each game, the jitters as I laced my cleats, was for her; wanting to outfox, outkick and outplay like a master and force her to notice me.

We played the richest school in our league two weeks after Bridget's birthday, a college whose alumni endowments paid for a gorgeous stadium and separate athletic center with locker rooms straight out of a five-star resort. Coach snorted; "Don't be intimidated by this shit. Nice towels in the locker room don't make you tougher on the field."

The opening whistle released the butterflies in my stomach, the roaring of lions in my head. But that night on the field we didn't play like lions, we played like tense women powered by anxiety instead of confidence. Bridget started strong but lost her mojo when they guarded Hanna effectively enough to block her from the game. If they had scored first it would have killed our morale, but we held them at bay, blocking their passes, kicking past their strategies, not anticipating their plays but countering them with desperate aggression.

Our forward Cady slid through a sudden opening and drove past their goalie, followed by screams of joy from the small cadre of students who'd come up on the bus. We mostly stayed silent, because we knew we were off our game. They came back down the field with renewed determination and it wasn't regionals I was thinking of but impressing Shea when I surged toward their forward. She looked surprised and angry to see me counter her so quickly; I tried to stop her from turning the ball and that was my last perception before the blue blur of her uniform and the sharp pain of a foot in my ribs.

I staggered and bent over. The ref's whistle cut through a hushed night. Bridget ran over to me as the arguments started about it being a yellow card. I held up a hand to show I was okay but it hurt to breathe.

"Just take a few." Shea was suddenly there, her arm around my back. "It's okay. We'll fucking kill them."

It was that quandary every athlete faces; shake it off like a pro and possibly compromise the team by playing at half-mast, or leave the field. Coach took me out, making the decision for me. The rest of the game was a bloodbath. Watching from the bench, I saw my team as the athletes they were, driving with aggressive dexterity, forcing the victory. We scored again, then a third time. Shutting out the rich school: it was a triumph.

But inside the fancy spa locker rooms, I went into one of the tiled showers and struggled not to cry. I felt shaky, not with that gratified postgame flush of triumph but a sense of letting everyone down.

Around me cascaded the pounding water of twenty other showers. My slippery shampoo bottle ejected out of my hand and outside the plastic curtain. I reached out for it and met eyes with Shea, wrapped in a white towel. Every shower stall curtain was pulled shut, the roar of water deafening.

She got into my stall and dropped her towel. The shower plastered her hair around her ears. We were naked together and the heat of her skin was palpable just inches from mine.

Her hands spanned my torso. "How bad is it?"

Her mouth was close to my ear, to talk over the water or to keep the rest of the team from hearing us, I didn't know.

"Bruised ribs. Nothing broken."

"Gonna have to get that bitch." She pushed me back against the tiles and kissed my mouth. It was the pinnacle of so many locker room dreams, Shea's weight on me, warm and slippery, overpowering me in all her butch, mysterious glory. We were kissing avidly, her fingers oddly gentle on my nipples, taking her time before her hand slid between my legs. Was she being gentle because I was injured or was she always this sensual and considerate? I didn't know.

"Don't stop kissing me when you come," she said. "I want to feel it in your mouth."

Feel what in my mouth? But I did; I felt it all, her fingers moving in my cunt and my ass, her wet nipples against mine, her tongue in my mouth, and a molten supernova rising up through my body. She took my ass in her hands and pulled me against her, rubbing her pussy against mine until I couldn't tell whose clit was whose, our skin fused and locked together in a rhythmic movement of wet friction. Shea fucking me into a searing, helpless animal cry that I muffled by sinking my teeth into her wet shoulder.

She took my hair in her fist and pulled back my head to kiss me again. Her fingers pushed inside me and worked me inside and out, filling me and teasing my clit until I moaned into her mouth, as anguished as I was excited by the unbearable need screaming in my blood. We slid down onto the tiles and she opened my legs wide, fucking my ass and pussy until a warm flood of bliss exploded inside me, spreading out in waves that resonated in my nipples, my stomach, my mouth.

She pulled back and laughed softly. "One day you can return the favor." She bit my lower lip hard, laughed again and wrapped her towel around her, exiting through the curtain.

The bus ride home was a festival of victorious whoops and replays, Cady passing around her vegan oatmeal cookies. Shea and I stayed solitary in the dark in separate seats with our headphones on, watching the highway pass.

All too soon I awoke to frost in spiderweb patterns on the windowpane: the harbinger of the end of soccer season. Tonight was the tournament where we would play Lana's school.

And *all too soon* was what everyone would say later about

that tournament. There just hadn't been enough time to show what we could do that season, not before the whistle blew and we launched into passing, kicking, grunting aggression, the lights blazing in our eyes and the screams from the crowd in our ears as we slipped past our enemies, intent on scoring. But one girl on the field was more intent than any of us, intent on vengeance, which is how Lana got the ball and took it down the field into what should have been a badly miscalculated gamble against Shea, the best goalie in the league. A gamble that turned into a kick, mistimed or perfectly timed, that landed with a foot in Shea's knee and a ball in our goal. And my magnificent butch goalie on the ground, cradling her leg with a tortured face that told everyone our season was over.

Home for winter break, I drove up to my high school a few days after Christmas and walked around my old soccer field where I had experienced the thrill of heading to state two years in a row. My best high school memories had happened here: playing next to high green cornfields on the glaring hot days of August, then the cooler days of fall when we practiced under gray Midwestern skies while students put together homecoming floats in the adjacent parking lot. But today a snowstorm had buried the lacrosse, soccer and football fields in a blanket of white and only a harsh wind was howling where I had once played to cheers of adulation.

My phone buzzed: Bridget. *Are you back yet? We're all going to the bar tonight.*

I drove back to school after dinner and was at the main off-campus bar by ten. Bridget, Hanna and a few of the others were in a booth in the back, the amber light turning their faces warm and soft. Hanna slid over and I sat down, my stomach jolting as I took in Shea across from me.

She permitted herself a small rare smile as Bridget poured me a beer. It was an off-season night for sure, several pitchers of beer on the table as everyone analyzed the College Cup game: who had stumbled, who had gotten lucky, who gave up a goal that should have been stopped. I tried to ignore Shea's leg against mine under the table. I couldn't tell if it was the shattered knee she'd had surgery on.

"At least you've got next year," Bridget said to me, a little enviously.

"A year without Shea," I said. Her hazel eyes met mine.

They assured me that there was already a great new goalie transferring in, that our chances were good next season. But that was a lie and everyone knew it. Everyone in the booth had spent probably the last ten years of her life dreaming of official soccer glory, championships, a shot at the women's Olympics or national team, girlhood dreams fed by coaches and sideline screams. And now we were in our twenties and turning into women who knew those dreams were done.

"Speaking of," Shea said, awkwardly getting out of the booth. "I gotta head home before the beer hits my leg."

Cady gasped. "Are you drinking on painkillers?"

Shea scoffed; no painkillers for her, she let us know, she could stoically suffer through any pain. But then she limped forward— pointedly, it seemed to me—and I finished my beer and stood up.

"I should get going too. I can help you if you need it."

It took a few minutes to make it out of the bar, three girls stopping Shea to coo over her knee and tell her what a hero she was, and then the bouncer stopping us to tell Shea that she was one fuck of an athlete and he'd admire her forever. College athletics: a time warp but a powerful one. Walking up the sidewalk, the snow shoveled into banks on either side, I could see that Shea's life after college was going to be much more of an adjustment than mine would be. Maybe that was why she said, "Let's walk up to the field."

She pulled me to her with one arm and leaned on me as we walked onto campus, past the brick dorms now darkened and quiet over winter break, and toward the soccer field. Snowflakes began to spiral down. I helped her onto the bleachers and we faced what should have been the ghosts of our team just two months ago. But the field was an alien landscape, devoid of sweat, glory, war or victory.

The snow looked lavender in the moonlight.

"It could have been different," Shea said. "But I don't know how much it matters."

She kissed me with sudden aggression, the strong warmth of her tongue contrasting with her cold fingers sliding under my sweater. I went still, a drumming in my heart spreading the visceral knowledge through my blood that she owned me at this moment. She stripped me down, pulling off my jacket and sweater and taking down my jeans. Then she pushed me back and regarded me in my underwear with a predatory smile.

My black lace bra was wet with snow, my nipples hard and pushing against the cups. She hooked a finger under the front band and yanked it up, catching my tits in her hands.

"Pull your underwear down and show me your pussy. Sit down on your jacket and open your legs for me."

I obeyed, shivering, mostly naked now in the winter night. She loomed over me with an impassive face, snowflakes catching on her hard cheekbones. The January breezes made me feel acutely how wet and swollen my pussy was.

She slowly rubbed my clit. Waves of heat swept down my skin. "Play with your tits," she ordered. "Give me a show while I fuck you."

I pushed them together and pulled on my nipples, making them stiffer and pinker. She didn't take her eyes off me, sliding one finger inside me, just an inch, and circling until I wiggled impatiently beneath her.

She laughed. "You little slut... But okay, I'll be nice."

She fell back on the bleachers, pulling me onto her until she was sucking the tips of my breasts. I sighed with relief and pleasure, the snowflakes falling gently on my back making her that much warmer and more solid beneath me. She muttered something like, "All you girls just want to get fucked and come..." and then roughly yanked me upward again until I was sitting on her face, her mouth like a hot snake moving under my cunt.

I was shivering hard with heat and excitement and snow, my body almost steaming in the night. Between my thighs, Shea looked unrecognizable from who she was on the field, her eyes half-open and glazed with bliss. Her short nails dug into my thighs but I turned around, reversing so I could run my hands over her thick muscled body.

This was what I wanted. I lifted her shirt and liberated her small tits, almost flat against her chest. I touched her nipples and continued down inside her jeans, feeling first the brown triangle of hair I'd seen in the shower and then her silky wetness, wetter than I'd have imagined stoic, brooding Shea would get. I half-forgot her tongue on my clit as I pushed her jeans down and buried my face in her cunt, the rich smell and taste of her, sweeter also than I would have guessed.

My tongue swam over her and her body jolted. When I sucked her pussy lips into my mouth she stopped attending to me entirely, rigid as I licked her and slid my fingers inside her. Her cunt walls quivered around my hand, so drenched it was all I could do not to pull out my fingers and lick them immediately, but I fucked her instead, slowly at first, feeling every inch of her. She moaned into my pussy, a noise of impatience and yearning, so I began fucking her properly, rubbing and twisting my fingers inside her.

She was shaking and kneading my thighs like a cat. It passed through my mind that Shea didn't let many people fuck her, that I was a rare visitor to her temple of vulnerability. And what a privilege it was to see my beautiful butch goalie melting and crying under my administrations, and then feel the storm in her body as her hips lifted and slammed down on the bleachers, wave after wave tightening around my fingers.

I was naked and wet in the falling snow on a January night. It hit me like a surprise, as if a spell had been broken. But Shea resurrected the spell with a grunt and brief push, attacking me from behind. She fingered me until I screamed, not caring if campus security came running to find two soccer players fucking each other on the bleachers in a blizzard, one naked and hoarse and freezing and burning in alternate waves by the second, my body on fire as if it had been waiting for Shea forever. The curious sensations of being incomplete and prolonged right on the edge, of needing to come for her, was like a raging thirst inside me, and then it broke and I was coming and crying as something like a glorious worship spilled out of my cunt.

My clothes were wet. I was a disaster. So was she. The security lights of campus blurred in my snowflake-clumped lashes as we got dressed and went to the warm showers of the athletic center.

"Maybe it had to be like this," Shea said, stretching under the water. She could have been talking about Lana, about us losing our season, about me losing her in an hour or a month. Maybe it was what she had to believe. I shut off my shower and dressed, drying my hair, and when I was done, she was waiting to walk me home.

TAMING MAY

Megan McFerren

May enters, clad in sun. Garlands of light drape and fall from her skin, left strewn in gold across the plush rug. Gossamer curtains curl and fan on the breeze through arched picture windows, and carry in the scent of lilacs hanging heavy from the walls outside. It renders the room luminous in a way May's never noticed before, soaking into the dense wood of the dining table, seeking into the secret spaces of the elaborate cornice molding encircling the room.

"Come."

Hannah's voice strips May to attention and centers her to the caress of woven scarlet carpet underfoot. The tea service blinks blindingly when she passes through swathes of sun, the silver tray heavy and cold against her hands. She does not yet look to the woman waiting poised at the head of the table, and instead demurs her gaze to the steaming pot and porcelain cups, the arrangement of biscuits circled around an ivory dish.

When she stops beside her, May's eyes rest upon the masculine riding boots that wrap leather warmth up Hannah's calves. Skintight cream breeches above, the long cascade of a velvet tailcoat—May wonders where she found it all, and her mouth tightens into a frown a moment too late for her to stop it.

"Speak."

May swallows down her displeasure, and resisting the trembling in her arms, extends the tea service a little farther.

"Your tea, madam."

"Not about the tea, darling girl," Hannah purrs. "Set it down."

The tray clicks to rest on the sprawling table, as empty now as the rest of the house with the usual family and attendants enjoying an afternoon picnic far out on the grounds. May withdraws her hands and presses them to her bare thighs, motionless but for a practiced patience in her breath. She makes a small sound when a thin stripe of black crosses the corner of her vision, and restrains the next noise as a fold of leather touches cold beneath her chin.

"Look at me." Hannah raises the crop, lifting May's face to meet her own. In an instant, May drinks her in, the flaxen hair knotted elegantly at the back of her neck, the high collar pressed stiff against her strong jaw. Her eyes are an endless darkness, glimmering with light, and to look into them is to seek the bottom of a well. "What have I done to earn such displeasure?"

"There was no displeasure, madam."

Hannah tips her chin aside, and her pink peony smile unfurls into bloom.

"No?"

"No, madam."

"You're lying," Hannah says. May's chest tightens, and even without the spill of sun across her freckles, her cheeks warm. "Twice, now, I've asked you to tell me. Twice now you've argued. I would not suggest pursuing it thrice."

May's breath leaves her all at once, and she curls her hands together at the small of her back. "I was surprised to see you dressed for riding," she manages.

"You frowned, darling, did you think I'd miss it?" A threat ripples like a shadow beneath Hannah's words.

"I was dismayed to see you dressed for riding," May corrects, embarrassed. Her fingers tighten against each other to fight back the urge to close her eyes. "It struck me as out of place to take tea in that way."

When Hannah laughs, pitching her head back in delight, it cracks sharp through the silence so carefully preserved.

"As if it were the only thing that will strike you," she grins. She lets the promise hold, pressing broad white teeth to her bottom lip, and then smooths her expression. The riding crop, unyielding, pushes May's chin higher. "What charming hypocrisy, to judge my garments when you yourself have none. And during tea, no less," Hannah chides.

She lets the whip drift downward, tracing the curve of May's throat. Despite the summer heat, the stroke of oiled leather between her breasts shivers her, hardening her nipples and tightening between her legs. Were she permitted to move, May would close her thighs firmly and squeeze. Were she permitted to move, May would spread her belly over Hannah's knees and grasp the legs of her chair. She would beg, to have now what she knows in a flutter of anticipation is coming.

"Patience," Hannah tells her, and May blinks in surprise to hear her desires so directly addressed.

"I'm sorry—"

Hannah taps the crop against May's thigh, hardly enough to make a sound, but more than what May needs for goose bumps to erupt across her skin.

"Serve."

May moves with caution. The cup and saucer first. The biscuits next, and the empty plate to accompany. May knows well this service, used at countless teas and luncheons. She has seen them since she was a little girl. She knows just as well that Hannah takes two sugar cubes, set without sound into the cup with impractically tiny tongs sized only for that purpose. There is an order and a form, in every turn of wrist to spread the offering before her mistress, and in every muscle that tightens up the stretch of bare thighs to her ass. Grasping the teapot, May pours a steady stream that seems to mirror the heat running through her veins, rising to steam on her sigh as she sets it back in place. A tip of milk is added, blooming pale—no more than that.

It has been a lesson hard learned, over stolen afternoons when they are free enough to play. May's skin aches with the memory of stripes and slaps that have left their mark to ensure the ritual is flawless, without effort, though it takes every part of her to make it seem so.

With a sleek slip of one leg over the other, Hannah brings the crop again to touch May's inner knee. There it rests, and May thinks she feels it tapping a quick tempo, only to find that Hannah holds it motionless and it is her own pulse rising instead.

"Is something wrong, madam?"

"Tell me what you want," Hannah answers, a curl of amusement in her words.

May presses her tongue between her lips to wet them, mouth dry.

"To serve, madam."

Flat leather finds the inside of one thigh, and then the other, pressing insistently. May works her heels outward, toes following, to widen, farther and farther. Still hovering bent across the tea service, she fears that if she continues to spread her legs, she will spill out her whole being onto the floor. The warm air cools her thighs, revealing how damp they've become, and a fierce blush blossoms unbidden over the swells of her body.

"Stop," Hannah says, and May shifts not a muscle beyond her hammering heart. Not until a snap of the crop against her leg curls her fingers against the table, not until a quick flick against the other forces her to swallow the moan that begs to break free. "Answer properly. You know better."

"I wish to learn how to serve you, madam," May breathes. Head bowed, her sable hair hangs in curls around her face, unbound, released from the tidy braid that normally holds it tamed. When a gloved finger slips a lock behind her ear, it is as shocking as a strike, and every bit as tender.

"Tell me why."

"I wish to learn how to serve you, madam, because you are wise in the ways of service and generous to teach me," May breathes, all at once like a breeze that lifts the curtains to nearly the ceiling.

Hannah strokes the backs of her knuckles, clad in kid-leather, down the knobs of May's spine, and as if by doing so fills her lungs with air, only to push it back out when her hand teases upward again.

"I am that, darling," agrees Hannah. "I've not spent my days idle like some spoiled girls, who lounge about doing little and thinking less."

May watches the woman's boots grind against the carpet as she stands and circles behind her. Toes first, twisting slightly, to leave behind a halo of earth. May knows Hannah hasn't been riding. She couldn't have been, and certainly not with the whole assorted household out on the grounds. Another step flakes soil from the soft bend of leather, and this time, May doesn't frown, but can't stop herself from asking:

"Are those mine?"

May's dark curls spill into the cruel grasp of Hannah's fingers. Shoved downward with a gasp, May bends until her stiff nipples harden near to numbness, brushing the table. The crop presents itself once more against her thigh, only a touch but enough to make May whimper, and when she tries to close her legs again Hannah's booted foot stops the movement.

The whisper of her breeches, the heat of her groin against May's ass is enough to pitch her whimper to a moan when Hannah leans heavily over her back. Leather stings hot against her thigh and May shifts to her toes to try and stretch the quivering muscle, but there is no give between Hannah's body and hers, hardly space enough to draw a breath.

"I'm sorry, madam," May pleads.

"You are a brat," whispers Hannah. "A spoiled, greedy brat."

"I want to serve—"

"But you don't—truly, you don't," Hannah says, voice lilting higher as she tightens her fist and turns May's head aside. "Had you your way, you'd spend it sitting here, in my chair—"

A strike, for emphasis, makes May's body rigid under her. The stripe of red tightens to a burn so hot it's nearly cold, and as the numbness passes it sends static discharge prickling sharp beneath her skin. May moans, unbidden, and her voice reverberates against the ancient wood beneath.

"Whose chair is it, darling?"

"Yours, madam," whispers May, her breath pooling pale against the table. Another clap of the crop lines her thigh.

"Whose house is this, darling?"

"Yours, madam!"

Another, crossed over to the other side as if spurring a racehorse on to victory.

"And whose boots are these, darling girl?" Hannah purrs, ducking her head to sweep a kiss across May's shoulder as she sobs in gratitude.

"Yours, madam."

May's fingers curl shaking against the table and she shifts her weight under Hannah. She stretches backward to meet the slow undulations of Hannah's hips rubbing against her. She leans forward to find the fine hairs between her legs parted by a bit of intricate decor carved into the table. It's enough to grind against, rocked slowly by Hannah's steady thrusts. It's enough that May's cheeks, already ruddy, darken to a torrid scarlet when she feels a wet trickle down her thigh.

The bliss of unyielding contact against her clitoris dizzies her when she rubs against the table. A moan betrays her bliss but rather than dealing another punishing snap of the crop for May's arrogance, Hannah's hand settles against her hip instead. The glove is cold, a startling contrast over heated skin, and in Hannah's palm the woven handle of the whip abrades, juxtaposed against gentle fingers.

"It is all mine. I am the one who has worked to make this place what it is," Hannah says, her voice a purr like that of a great cat, a tiger contented but with all the potential to lash out at any moment. "The boots and the chair, the house and you," she adds, and May does not need to see Hannah's grin to hear it in her words. "You especially."

"I am yours, madam."

"My beautiful serving girl," laughs Hannah. "My darling May."

The crop is set on the table, as if in warning for further disobedience. May sighs rattling relief, and with abandon shoves her hips back against Hannah's. Electricity twines sparking up her legs when Hannah's touch seeks trembling thighs, and bursts white behind her eyes when Hannah parts May's lips to stroke her fingers through her maid's wetness.

Only a fingertip penetrates, a teasing little touch, not nearly enough to satisfy the coiling tension in May's belly. Pressure winds sinuously from her pussy, shortening her breath and spurring her pulse, and May fears only distantly the return of others to the house. Hannah would not risk being caught this way, no more than May herself—indeed, the retribution that both would suffer would be unconscionable, and so May trusts, as she always has, in Hannah's wisdom.

If she deems May's service unacceptable, she will tell her.

If she decides that May is better bared or dressed, she will make certain that she knows how she prefers her to be.

And if there is time enough for this, then May can do nothing more than spread her legs a little farther in welcome and moan when Hannah works a damp, gloved finger inside of her.

Cold leather warms in the heat of her body. As if her fingers were a cock, Hannah grinds her hips forward and pushes deeper inside, opening May's cunt. She is already wide with wanting, dripping embarrassingly slick over Hannah's hand, and she looks across her shoulder to the woman mounting her. Freckles dapple Hannah's cheeks in the sun, her hair unwound around her face from the effort of taming May. Lips swollen with desire, parted flushed and panting, she is lovely, and May finds herself as breathless in seeing Hannah take her as she is in being claimed.

A second finger joins the first, thrusting her enough to jostle the tea setting where it sits untouched. Whimpering, May lifts a shaking hand to Hannah's in her hair. It loosens, their fingers join and May drags Hannah's hand against her mouth. Her breath swells hot back against her lips as she groans her adoration into Hannah's palm, nearly laughing when Hannah closes her fingers over May's mouth, enough to restrict her breath but not to stop it. May's legs shake under the rhythmic, rough fucking against the table; she pushes to her toes as if to join her body with the way her heart reels higher, faster, spinning to dizzying heights.

Hannah's fingers curl inside of her, rubbing against the little bulb inside that would level May to her knees if not for Hannah holding her in place. Her voice rises, pitching into shorter gasps, until a helpless cry takes her and the tightness, rigid in her body, breaks. Like a rope pulled too tight, May snaps and uncoils, the reverberations of her release rocking her body in echoes that roll from her throat to her toes and back again.

Even when Hannah works her fingers free, May still ruts against the table, a mindless motion of joyous, animal pleasure.

She knows who owns her.

And just as May is certain she could not love Hannah more, she strokes her fingers across May's damp, parted mouth and grasps her chin, to turn the girl to face her. Bare backside against the table, gloved hand between her legs again, May slips her arms around Hannah's neck and nuzzles the stiff collar of her shirt.

"Keep me," May begs her, delirious with delight and fondness both.

"Always," Hannah promises. "Always, darling." She smooths May's wild curls from her face and claims her with a kiss.

When her family returns, her mother greets her first, as servants bustle past the dining room with the remains of their picnic. "Sweetheart, we missed you terribly. The weather was simply lovely. Your father resigned himself to reading beneath a tree, so he didn't join us in croquet. More's the better, as I was able to win without him knocking the balls off across the field."

Brisk steps carry her to where May sits at the head of the table, dressed in a soft white cotton shift meant for sleeping.

"I'm just taking tea," May responds, as her mother sets a hand to her brow.

"You're not feverish," she says, before pressing a palm to May's cheek. "Are you feeling better?"

May offers a smile, and lifts the cup to her lips. The tea is cold but sweet, and not only because of the two cubes of sugar within. Past her mother, she shares a smile with Hannah, standing with the other maids and clad once more in her somber dark dress and white pinafore. She looks away only when Hannah grins, and May's thighs ache in memory of being taught again who is truly in ownership here.

May's cheeks warm, from a fever all her own.

"Yes," she agrees. "Much better."

CRÈME BRÛLÉE

Sacchi Green

"Hey Rory, somebody's asking for you. Knows your name."

I saw the sly grin on Audrey's face, saved my spreadsheet and quit Excel. "I don't think it's a complaint," she called to my retreating back.

I wasn't focusing on the accounts anyway, just daydreaming. Remembering someone I'd never see again, didn't want to see, because I'd never be able to resist her. The only person in years who could melt me inside the shell I'd constructed so carefully, and break right on through it. Just that one night, around this time last year...

And there was Raf, in the very solid flesh, seated in the same alcove overlooking the salt marsh. I felt her magnetism all the way across the dining room. Last year I'd bribed Audrey to let me wait on that table; this time I didn't even bother to snatch her order pad.

The broad back, the granite-gray hair clipped short, could have belonged to any of thousands of guys vacationing on Cape Cod—or hundreds of women, this close to Provincetown. But I knew exactly who it was. Knew every line and curve and hollow of the body beneath the slate-blue jacket and white shirt, not to mention the gray slacks. I'd explored all of her well enough to make sketches from memory, and to chisel and polish her image out of pink Cadillac Mountain granite from Maine.

"Good evening," I said, demurely, just as I had the first time. "I'm Rory. I'll be serving you tonight."

Raf kept her gaze on the menu spread out across the white tablecloth, but her mouth twitched and then expanded into a wide grin. "I'll have my usual," she said, and lifted those clear hazel eyes to me. I could barely keep my own lips steady.

"Two appetizers to share? Wellfleet oysters on the half-shell and ceviche of Chatham scallops?" I looked pointedly at the empty chair across from her. A year ago it had been nicely filled indeed by a voluptuous young thing trying to obey her dyke Daddy's instructions to eat the raw shellfish whether she wanted to or not. I'd taken pity and told the girl that the lime juice in the ceviche more or less "cooks" the scallops. "And two entrées, the bouillabaisse and the cioppino? With the house white zinfandel, black coffee, no dessert?" I'd be damned if I'd ask about the girl. What was her name? Juliana?

"Actually, I was kind of looking forward to dessert."

My blood had been simmering. Now it came to a slow boil, remembering how we'd gone at each other like starving wildcats in my studio at 2:00 A.M. when Juliana was safely asleep at their motel, exhausted after an evening of clubbing in Provincetown.

"But for the rest," Raf went on, "just one appetizer and entrée, unless I can get you to share with me. Would your boss allow that?"

"I'm the boss tonight. Technically, the assistant manager." Which didn't guarantee that I'd get away with it. Audrey could be bribed, but there were six other waitresses, already intensely interested in what I was up to. Tough. It wouldn't be easy to replace an assistant manager who also did the accounting. Not this late in the season. "And as the boss, I happen to know that the duck in beach plum-Cabernet sauce is especially good tonight. I'll go for the oysters, but duck instead of bouillabaisse." Raf already knew that I'm far from the submissive type, but the emphasis on choosing my own meal wouldn't hurt.

I caught Audrey's eye and motioned her to the table to take our order. Then I swept the room with a steely gaze that got the rest of the waitresses hustling the way they were supposed to.

"I went by your studio and the gallery," Raf said, as soon as we'd been supplied with ice water and lemon slices. "I was hoping you'd be there, covered in clay dust like you were last summer."

Daddy and girl had wandered from the co-op gallery into my studio, clearly looking for a corner just secluded enough to pretend no one could see them making out. The girl's shorts had been so brief they revealed rosy traces of the proprietary bar code Daddy's hand had imprinted on her naughty ass. They must have indulged in a bit of after-lunch action before taking a stroll through the galleries.

Juliana had pouted when they'd seen me there, but Raf had chatted, admired my stone and porcelain nudes, stroked a tempting set of smooth marble buttocks and probed a big finger down between the irresistible thighs. My crotch got wet enough to dampen the clay dust layering my jeans. When they turned up later at the restaurant where I work to earn the minimal living that art can't provide, it felt like the truck that had hit me had stopped to take me for a ride.

The way Raf looked at me now in my conservative pantsuit made me sure she was thinking more of how I'd looked later that night covered in nothing at all. Just the way I was remembering her.

"I've been working more in stone than clay since then. Still get covered in dust, though."

"I noticed some of your new sculptures, there and in that

fancier gallery up the hill." She hesitated. "That piece in the pink-speckled stone...with the NOT FOR SALE sign..." Her sun-ruddy face got a little redder. She would never have seen herself from the angle I'd portrayed; rear view, recumbent, quarter-scale, with smooth flesh emerging out of a jagged granite base. Broad shoulders, the side-swell of a breast, head turned to the right, just a few details of face and brush-cut hair...the effect was on the verge of being abstract, but clearly inspired by a real person. And she knew it.

"That's brought me a couple of commissions," I said, with studied casualness. "Thanks for the inspiration. Who'd have thought anyone rich enough to afford it would want a stylized portrait of her lover in stone? Maybe I'll be able to make a living with my art one of these days after all."

The oysters arrived just in time to save Raf from having to figure out what to say. I enjoyed the hell out of her discombobu-lation. Let her wonder whether I'd been using her for my own artistic purposes rather than succumbing to pure lust.

But then I blurted out, "I'll never sell that one." So much for staying cool and detached.

"I'm glad." Raf plucked an oyster on its half shell from the bed of ice chips and raised it toward me like a salute before tilting the sweet juice into her mouth. I did the same. We managed a simultaneous sliding of the oysters themselves across our tongues and down our throats, swallowing in perfect synchronization, then licking our lips. And grinning.

"The sauce is worth trying, too." I spooned a bit of chipotle mignonette onto another oyster, then licked it slowly off before sucking the slippery morsel into my mouth.

"Mmm." Raf tried it, even more dramatic in her licking and sucking. "Not bad, but not the very best sauce I've ever tasted."

A sound at my shoulder like stifled laughter erupted into a snort. Audrey, bringing the scallops ceviche in their little avocado boat. I pretended not to have heard. As soon as she left Raf raised a questioning eyebrow and jerked her head in the direction of Audrey's sashaying butt.

I shook my head. "Audrey's a good kid in her way, but a one-trick pony, and that trick is getting her posterior paddled by any means necessary. Once in a while I'll indulge her, but I make her earn it. Last time you were here that's how I bribed her to let me wait on your table. There's nothing more between us."

We finished off the last two oysters sedately, though we were close to laughter, before turning to the contrast of tender scallops tangy with lime and jalapeño and the buttery luxury of perfectly ripened avocado. I could almost forget the memory of young Juliana sampling the same dish with a high degree of suspicion.

Raf must have thought of Juliana, too, or maybe she read my mind. "Funny how much better food tastes when you're with someone who really knows how to enjoy it."

I still wouldn't ask about the girl. "Maybe we should have ordered lobster, too, for the full *Tom Jones* effect."

"That's exactly it! When I said something along those lines to Juliana, she had no idea what I was talking about. Never heard of *Tom Jones* the movie, much less the book, or even the singer who lifted the name."

"Ah, youth," I said. "Just the same, she's certainly a tasty bit of arm candy for a stroll around Provincetown."

"She was, wasn't she?"

Past tense. So my first unasked question was answered.

And then the second. "We outgrew each other. At least I outgrew her, and she transferred to a West Coast college." She shrugged. "It was about time."

The intensity in her hazel eyes as she watched for my reaction was my cue to ask what it was time for now. A second frantic, earthshaking fuck with me, and then on to the next sweet young morsel who wanted to act out fantasies of submission with the biggest, baddest gray-fox butch around? The fuck I would make sure of. The rest I'd just as soon skip.

The entrees arrived just in time to save me from having to respond. "It's not too late to add some lobster," I said.

Raf grinned but shook her head. "Better not bite off more than we can chew." She plucked a mussel from the cioppino tureen, yanked open its shell with her fingers and ran her tongue around the interior. I joined in the game with a quick twist to tear duck leg from duck thigh, brandishing the drumstick at her before sinking my teeth into the meatiest part. Purple plum sauce ran down my chin and hand.

"How about a baby calamari?" She held one out on her fork and made the tentacles seem to dance in the air. I almost wished Juliana had been there after all so I could watch her reaction.

"Aw, how cute." I held out the duck leg with the bite I'd taken out of it uppermost. "Slip it right into there." The tiny cephalopod made it from fork to drumstick to my mouth. It went as well with my plum sauce and pecan pilaf side dish as it would have with the cioppino broth.

Even in the alcove we weren't all that secluded. Several nearby observers were taking an interest in our antics, so we toned it down a bit and concentrated more seriously on our food.

All this time I'd stayed aware of what went on in the dining room and in the bar beyond. Customers waiting for tables were bunching up in the bar, so I licked sauce off my fingers, left purple streaks across the white linen napkin, and went to straighten things out. An annex usually reserved for small private parties was opened up, tables were set, and the standby waitress helping out at the bar was assigned to cover them. I went back to Raf.

"Doesn't look like you'll be getting off early tonight," she observed, and took a sip of wine.

"Not unless I want to settle for a quickie in the ladies' room, which I don't. The pink and powder-blue décor does nothing for me."

Raf nearly choked on the wine. I thought for a few seconds that I might need to demonstrate my Heimlich maneuver skills.

The prospect of squeezing my arms around her from behind had a certain carnal attraction, but she recovered soon enough and mopped her face with her napkin, only slightly spotted with tomato sauce from the cioppino.

"Well then," she said after drawing a few deep breaths, "when *do* you expect to get out of work? In time for a jaunt into P-town? Or a walk on some beach?"

I opened my eyes wide in mock astonishment. "You mean, like, a real date?"

Raf didn't miss a beat. "Nothing wrong with a change of pace now and then."

"You have a point there. I moved to Wellfleet to leave behind the distractions of P-town-and-Gomorrah and focus on my art, but it might be fun to stroll along Commercial Street with the brand of arm candy that gives all the baby-femmes wet dreams."

"I'm sure you inspire plenty of wet dreams yourself." The look in her eyes would have made her meaning clear even if she hadn't laid her big hand over mine on the table.

"There's a market among the young set for weathered androgyny like mine, too," I conceded, staying deliberately casual but not withdrawing my hand. "Especially if I make an effort to look extra mean and tough. But it was getting to be more trouble than it was worth."

"I know just what you mean." She drew her hand back and finished off her wine. "So how about we try the old-fashioned way and get to know each other. You close here when? Ten o'clock?"

"Nine. Wellfleet doesn't keep Provincetown hours. Where should I pick you up? If we meet at my studio we might not get any farther after all."

She told me where she was staying, we finished off what food we felt like bothering with and I got back to managing the increasingly busy restaurant. Just before nine I slipped into the kitchen and wheedled the cook into letting me take two special desserts in their white pottery ramekins and a container of ice to keep them chilled. The bartender, who owed me several favors, agreed to handle closing up.

On the long stretch from Wellfleet through Truro to Provincetown Raf and I chatted like blind dates feeling each other out, while repressing the urge to feel each other up.

"What made you decide to be a sculptor? Especially with stone?"

"Oh, I started out with clay pots, mugs, that sort of thing. Pretty commercial in tourist season. But stone...maybe it's the challenge. To feel the shape a piece could have, then cut and chisel and grind and polish until by my own strength and sweat and profanity I get the right balance between what I want and what the stone can take. When it really works out, there's a rush like nothing else."

Raf started to speak, paused, then came out with it. "Sounds like the mother of all power trips."

"Oh, yeah." I wasn't offended. "And the best thing about stone is that it's solid. Cut or bore or chisel into it, and it's stone all the way down. You need to recognize the grain, and sometimes striations, but there's no soft core with chaotic feelings or longings or resentments." Maybe I was revealing too much. Maybe I wanted to.

"Looks like you almost always choose to sculpt naked women. Or just parts of them." Raf wasn't pulling any punches either.

"Is there any sculptor who doesn't? And they sell."

"Yours are something special. And you don't always sell them. Do you...well, do you use many models?"

"Can't usually afford models. But I have an excellent memory." Enough of that. "So how about you? What do you do besides instruct young beauties in the finer points of sex and submission?"

Raf hesitated. "You know what? Let's skip the P-town scene and go walk and talk on a beach."

So we didn't make it to the bars and crowds after all. From Pilgrim Heights where Route 6 starts downhill, the bright lights along the hook-shaped shore of Provincetown made a pattern so lovely it was better not to spoil it by getting too close. Instead, we veered off toward Race Point where we walked barefoot on the sand by moonlight, watching waves roll slowly in under starry skies. As clichéd as it gets and too windy for much conversation, but exhilarating. It was good to be sharing something exhilarating besides sex.

Eventually we found a sheltered spot in the dunes. We could still hear the waves, and the stars looked even brighter as the moon sank lower.

Raf settled her butt into the sand and began to talk. "I work as a supervisor for the Post Office, currently in central Vermont. Nice country, but kind of isolated in many ways." She paused.

"I know the quarries up around there," I said, to fill the silence. "Some of the best marble in the world. I can't afford the perfect stuff, but I go there to look for broken slabs or pieces with faults. I like the challenge of making the imperfect stones into something special."

"Hey, that's great! Call me next time you're heading that way. Stay with me. I mean...I don't want to lose you this time."

It was too dark to be sure, but I had the impression that she was blushing. Then she went on. "There are quite a few married dykes in Vermont trying to make it in farming or arts and crafts, but... At least Boston is within reach. My ex and I broke up when we both felt like we'd become different people."

I put a not-quite-comradely arm around her solid back. "Yeah, I know how those things go."

Raf followed my comradely arm routine. We wriggled even closer to each other. "There's a club in Boston, women-only BDSM."

"Yeah, I've heard of it." I mentioned the name. "I know a couple of the founders, but they drifted away when the members got too involved in wrangling about bylaws and business meetings and so forth. "

"Well, that's where I found out that old-school butches of a certain age were back in style. Or maybe they never went out of style in the city. Whatever, the youngsters were lining up for some good old-fashioned domination, and giving them what they wanted came naturally to me. It was...great, for quite a while. Intoxicating."

"Was?" No guarantee needed. I just wondered.

"Maybe. I don't know. It gets to be so much work, fulfilling their fantasies, being who they want me to be, not getting...not getting what you and I had last year. I couldn't get you out of my mind."

"My mind isn't the only place that remembers you." I slid my hand along her thigh. Cocksure or, as now, on the verge of vulnerable, Raf still had that aura, that presence, whatever it was that grabbed me hard and made my depths clench. She turned, enveloped me in those strong arms...and an arc of headlights swept across the top of the dune and skimmed her gray hair. New arrivals, and from the sounds they weren't here just to stay in their car and make out.

I sighed, then sighed again more deeply, enjoying the way the motion rubbed my breasts against her chest.

"Maybe we're too mature to roll around in the sand here, anyway," she said.

"I guess. Just like we're mature enough to get the most out of playing with our food." I tried to get disentangled. "Come on back to the car. I brought dessert."

Raf's hand cupped my ass to help me up. "But I thought you were going to be my dessert!"

"That'll be second dessert. And again for first breakfast. This is different."

The newcomers were busy building a driftwood fire on the beach. I moved my car to the far end of the parking lot. In the glow of the overhead light I leaned over into the back to get my treasures out of their chilly container. Raf took the opportunity to knead my upturned butt and tease between my thighs, but with a steel-willed effort I got the ramekins safely onto a towel folded on the front seat.

"Crème brûlée!" I said triumphantly. "Have you ever had it?"

"Just seen it on restaurant menus a time or two. What's it mean? Bruised cream?"

"Intriguingly kinky, but no. More like broiled cream. The top is covered with raw sugar, melted under a broiler or a propane torch, and then it hardens like glass." I dug some plastic spoons out of the side pocket on the door where I shove them when I get drive-through coffee.

"Dig in." I knew what would happen. Raf's spoon splintered on the golden surface.

"You're the stonecutter in this crew. You do it."

I took out my pocketknife, covered it in plastic wrap that had protected the desserts, and brought it down hard on one sugar-glazed portion. Cracks rayed out, revealing glimpses of the inner custard. "That's yours. Now you break my shell."

She did it with one hand, while the other pulled my head close for a long, sensuous kiss. Finally she leaned back. "So, did I break through?"

"Oh yeah." I couldn't remember whether we'd done anything as slow and sweet as kissing last year. I was breathless. "No shell left at all."

"Looks like some crunchy bits left." She scooped up some of the rich creamy custard along with fragments of sugar glaze. "Mmm. Now I know what you see in this. Such rich, smooth cream inside that stony exterior." She took another bite, then offered me one. We alternated with the spoon, feeding each other, until the last bites were accidentally-on-purpose smeared across our lips. The licking and kissing that followed got us too revved up to drive all the way back to Wellfleet without relief, so I pulled off at the Pilgrim Springs Trail parking lot, mercifully unoccupied.

I won the race to get each other's clothes off. My wiry build let me twist and wriggle, so I had her chest binding loosened and my hands full of breasts rejoicing in their freedom before she got under my sports bra. She chewed her way down my neck and shoulder and made me arch backward when her mouth got to my nipples, even as I was working my hand under her loosened belt and into the warm, pungent mysteries below.

The car was too cramped for all we needed, but the National Seashore provides sturdy picnic tables. I feasted first, kneeling on pine needles while Raf leaned back against the table. I got her slacks down far enough to access the coppery bush I remembered, although there was no telling in the dark whether it was still untouched by gray. All that mattered was her creamy tang, the tension of her straining clit when my tongue lashed at it, the clenching of her muscles around my fingers deep inside her and the full-throated cry that came when her spasms of release shook the wooden boards so hard they creaked.

Then it was my turn to press my naked ass against the hard-edged table while Raf's strong hands pinched and kneaded and made all my tenderest parts quiver with pleasure close to pain. At last I moaned, "Inside! Deep!" and when she obliged, my hips tilted to meet the pressure, demanded more, and I rode her hand until stars exploded out of my center to hang in the night sky above me, brighter than all the galaxies in the distant Milky Way.

For all that, we were more than ready to start over when we made it back to Wellfleet. "I don't actually live at my studio," I told Raf. "I have a perfectly good bedroom in a little saltbox house down the road." But she voted for the studio again, out of nostalgia, so we rolled out my old futon and went at it as though our two bodies would consume each other, driven by a common weight of years, of life, of howling pleasure into the teeth of mortality.

This time she didn't have to leave at sunrise. "This is what, fourth dessert? Or first breakfast?"

I stretched a bit stiffly and rubbed against her. She seemed to have acquired a scratch mark or two on her flanks where I sleepily recalled gripping her hard in extremity. "I'm not sure, but it won't be long before 'bruised cream' is the right term after all. And that's just fine with me." Things had never been finer, in fact. I felt another sculpture coming on, in creamy marble this time. And maybe a few small faults along its sides for added interest.

BUSH GARDEN

J. Belle Lamb

With thanks to Ginuwine's "Pony"

Susie's not tending bar tonight. It's got you on edge as you order drinks from the cocktail server, whose smile is pleasant enough. Still, she's not Susie, and the sense of something different, the nagging edge of something out of place, a pulled thread or an eyeliner smudge, is distracting. You've been coming to Bush Garden for years precisely because it doesn't change. The pistachio-green sinks in the restrooms: still the same as when they were installed in the '70s. The drinks: still awful if you don't order call liquor. The curved vinyl banquettes and brass-edged rolling chairs: still too dirty if you look closely, and still as full of laughing patrons as every other time you've been here. The songs: still karaoke classics crooned by regulars who have been coming here for thirty years, and still a handful of adventurers from the city's hipper districts dropping a little Lady Gaga and the occasional Usher track into the mix.

Susie is usually part of the Bush Garden magic: crow's feet

at the edges of heavily mascaraed eyes that crinkle as she smiles while she shakes drinks in both hands at once. She remembers the name on every tab, and she's good enough to start mixing another round of drinks after catching your eye across the crowded bar. You sip your drink, a perfectly adequate vodka martini, and don't let yourself sigh.

After all, it's a good night. You're out with your girls: Tracy's sitting next to you, arm almost possessive as it lazes across the back of the banquette. She's been laughing and playing along as you've flirted with Jean-Marie. You stretch in your seat, feeling eyes slip over you from around the room. It's a pretty three-some you make, all piled together in the curved booth, wiggling against each other and trading seats as you tease back and forth, your icy-blonde curls and gray eyes a contrast to Jean-Marie's smooth, dark skin and Tracy's buttoned plaid and not-quite-buzz cut. You don't mind the eyes on you as you flick your own around the room, watching drinks slosh as other tables flip through the karaoke song list binders.

"Yo, Tray. You think this crowd would appreciate some T.I.?" Jean-Marie leans across you to talk to Tracy, breasts in scoop-neck T-shirt grazing yours as she stretches so that she can hear Tracy's response. You let your hand drift to rest on her thigh, tight denim warm under your hand. She and Tracy have been debating song choices for the past half hour, covering the table with a snowdrift of filled-out song slips. You filled yours out and handed it to the K-jay not long after you arrived. It's your usual song, a Dusty Springfield classic. The cold vodka briefly numbs your lips. You intend to keep drinking until you have to sing, and then keep the bright booze going until you can mostly forget that you sang. Susie understands. If she were here, she'd have a fresh martini waiting for you after the song.

But Susie isn't working tonight. Before you can scowl again at the cocktail server's back, Tracy's voice cuts through your clouded thoughts: "Hey, Trix, don't you know her?"

You follow Tracy's gaze to the woman laughing as she rises from a table across the room. You didn't hear the name the K-jay called, but it's true: you remember meeting the woman at a house party not long ago. "Yeah. I think that's Stella. We met her at Jay's house."

Jean-Marie settles back into her seat, rearranging the slips of paper on the table again. "She's kinda cute," she says, nodding at Stella as she steps up onto the little stage at the front of the room.

You smile, agreeing with Jean-Marie: Stella is attractive, chin-length dark curls framing high cheekbones and big, dark eyes. She's dressed to show off her lush curves tonight in a low-cut silk blouse over leggings with a red and orange scarf that lends warmth to her sandy-dark cheeks. But it's not her outfit, or the sparkle in Stella's eyes as she takes the mike from the K-jay that sends a wave of cheers through the bar. It's the quick half grind she does against the mike-stand as the song's opening bass beat drops, a low thrum overlain with a synthed-up deep voice that starts repeating: "Yeah...yeah...yeah..."

And then Stella rips into the song, lyrics about looking for a partner who knows how to ride. Recognition ripples through the bar as more and more people note the hip-hop tune, turned on its head as Stella digs into its classic grind. Her voice is incredible as she half growls, half coos in a honeyed alto that takes the already sexy hip-hop lyrics and makes them into a come-on that settles immediately into your cunt. You're wet so fast that the shock of it sends a tremor across the surface of the icy vodka as you hold the glass, drink forgotten when Stella began to sing.

"Holy shit," Jean-Marie says as she dances in her seat next to you, shoulders and hips picking up the beat. "That girl can sing!" You all three watch as Stella teases the tables closest to the stage with a glimpse of her cleavage.

Tracy's "Yay-ah" on your other side is hungry, and when you

glance at her, she's nodding her head in time to the beat, a wide grin rounding her cheeks.

You put your drink down, not trusting yourself with the stemmed glass, as Stella flips her curls back and brings the mike closer to red lips, beckoning to the crowd with two curled fingers as she sings about finding someone horny enough to ride her pony. A piece of paper flies through the air to land on the edge of the stage. You're positive it contains a phone number.

It's a brash song, every note woven through with sex, with the glitter and sweat of the thousand strip clubs where it's played since it hit the radio a decade ago. Stella, though, as she throws the lyrics over the crowded bar, has made it into a command: you will listen to her. And you will want her—not because she's shimmying as she sings, and not because your mouth has gone dry as you follow her eyes as they slide down to her swaying cleavage for a second before she turns them, glowing, back on the crowd, but because she's telling you that yeah, tonight she wants you to want her. And you do. You want Stella right now, want that voice in your cunt, want its slickness in yours, rich sound fucking you, filling you.

Sweat breaks out on the back of your neck as the song continues. The bar has gone crazy for Stella. Everyone is dancing or singing along, from the table of thirty-year regulars in scruffy sport coats and crumpled fedoras to the gaggle of stilettoed girls who just ordered a round of shots. Jean-Marie's breasts bounce as she's moving next to you, hands up as her hips swivel against the vinyl seat, dark eyes picking up Stella's heat. Even Tracy breaks her reserve, arm dropping from the back of the booth to rest against the upper curve of your ass, fingers tapping against you in time with the song's beat. You feel another bead of sweat spring up between your breasts and drip slowly down.

Gravity shifts with Stella as she draws the song up through her pelvis, voice making it every bit as clear as her hips' purl that she'd make good on the song's promises if given the chance. She uses her palm to trace her own curves, the inch of air between her hand and her body suddenly the place everyone in the bar wants to be as she sings about sending chills down your spine.

You close your eyes, trying to ignore the insistent buzz the song has stirred up in your cunt, but when you open them, you're suddenly trembling up there on the little stage with Stella, cheap spotlight filling your eyes with white fuzz as she pushes you down on a bar table. The song continues, synth bass and lyrics about *riding my pony* looping over and over. Stella's pushing your thighs open, your little black dress gone just as magically as the table appeared under you. She's naked, too, down to her red patent-leather pumps, bronze skin shimmering under the spotlight. Stella bends over, generous breasts skimming the insides of your thighs as she puts her red lips on your cunt. She's still singing, the lyrics dissolving into rich sound as her tongue slicks over your folds. Her voice wraps around your clit, honey and strip-club grind making your hips thrust to meet her song.

You blink in the fizzy white light and suddenly, Jean-Marie's there, too, dark brown breasts skimming bare over your ribs as she leans to lick the thin line of sweat from your cleavage. She lifts a hand to wrap around your throat as you tip your head back against the table, her mouth on your nipple and Stella's voice in your cunt creating twin whirlpools. The song rides on, saddle waiting, as Jean-Marie lets you lift your head just enough to glimpse Stella's bare ass swaying under the stage lights. It's only waiting for a second, though, and then the light crackles again and Tracy's there, her strap-on buckles glinting silver under the harsh light as she steps up behind Stella. Tracy's cock—it's the big cock, the one that leaves you bruised if she rams it into you as hard as you like—is ready as Stella thrusts herself back against it, rich sounds of her pleasure mixing with the song as her tongue reaches deep into your cunt. Your head falls back against the bar table's edge, vision blurring as you lose yourself in tongues, hands and bared flesh under the bright lights.

It seems to last forever, this perfect moment on the bar stage: Tracy's pink cheeks as she fucks Stella while Stella is bent over, voice buried in your cunt, and Jean-Marie sucking your nipple as she holds you down on the table, fucking herself with her free hand. You know you're moaning wildly as Stella's big breasts push into your thighs, her tongue digging deeper into your cunt, curling impossibly tight against your G-spot as the lyric drives into your clit, over and over again. Jean-Marie has her hand clapped tight over your mouth, keeping your screams from interrupting the song's backbeat. You can feel Stella's orgasm building as she cries into your cunt, Tracy's cock thrusting relentlessly into her, and Jean-Marie shaking against you as her own pleasure starts to peak.

It's a chain reaction, more like nuclear fusion than dominos falling: you can't tell if your gushing orgasm tips Stella over the edge, or if her long, low cry, as her cunt clutches Tracy's cock, kicks off a tidal wave. Or if Tracy's growl happens before or after Jean-Marie bites your breast, hard, as she comes. But come you all do, in sloppy, sweaty, shared orgasms that make the little bar table creak dangerously as it struggles to hold you up under cascading groans and sighs. You close your eyes against the white fuzz and slip under the backbeat, pony's hooves pounding, for what seems like forever.

You're dimly aware of wild applause around you, and even more dimly aware that your fingers hurt from gripping the edge of the table.

"You okay, babe?" Tracy's voice at your ear draws you the rest of the way back into your seat.

"Uh-huh." You can't make words, and you certainly can't begin to explain the lightning-hard orgasm that just ripped through you. Stella kicks a heel up in a playful "Who, me?" half curtsy as the bar continues to applaud. Condensation trickles down the sides of your martini glass as you feel sweat dripping down your back, under your black dress. Jean-Marie laughs and cheers as Stella moves through the crowd, collecting high fives.

"Beatrice! Come on up!" The K-jay's voice cuts through the crowd. You wave her off weakly, shaking your head so that she knows to call someone else up. You know you should force yourself to sing as you always do, but until you can slip off to the bathroom to mop up your sopping cunt, there's no way you're going up on that stage.

A COOKING EGG

Roxy Katt

Finally, the external character of work for the worker is shown by the fact that it is not his own work but work for someone else, that in work he does not belong to himself but to another person.

—Karl Marx, "Alienated Labor"
(from *Economic and Philosophical Manuscripts*)

Staring out the rain-spattered window, she looked as if she had spent her life staring out of rain-spattered windows.

The window was one of many on the second floor of a country seat that might have been straight out of *Brideshead Revisited*. Before the building was the grandiose driveway that made a circle before the mansion and then receded in a straight line way down a rolling hill through gardens and pollarded trees to the distant gates.

Look at me, the face behind the window seemed to say: this forty-something secretary with big, round glasses and voluminous black hair. But no one was looking.

Down below on the great circle of the driveway was Alexis the maid, talking to the new chauffeuse.

Brandy was her name. She was risking a cigarette in the waning precipitation just as the sun was threatening, but not quite daring, to come out. She leaned back with her tightly leather-panted ass on the wing-like fender of the ancient Silver Ghost. Even her grandmother would have been born after that car was made.

Odile's phone rang on her desk by her elbow and she answered it impatiently, still staring at the cow-skinned angel with the short burgundy hair. "Yes, yes. That's fine. Yes, that's it. No, it's all being outsourced to the East." She hung up.

Irrelevant interruptions.

Brandy was lean and firm and encased head to foot in rich, deep-brown leather: short, tightly buttoned jacket and high-waisted breeches. She had a thigh gap to die for, and the pants that showed it off so well were exquisite. For while they closed at the back with a zipper, and at the front there was a kind of square sailor flap, closed with buttons along the top. Along each side ran a thick, vertical zipper.

She was not particularly tall, but taller than the staring Odile: Odile with her dark eyes and her hunger.

Brandy was as fresh as the rain.

On one end of Odile's desk was a hot plate and a pot of simmering water with an egg in it. The egg would soon be rattling when the water boiled, and this made Odile's office seem cozy somehow. Just as Odile was about to turn away from the window, Brandy turned her eyes up and looked straight at her as if she had known all along Odile had been watching. She gave the older woman a dark and knowing smile that almost made her gasp, threw the butt of her cigarette on the driveway and ground it out.

Odile's lips parted slightly and she put a hand lightly to her throat.

Smiling, pulling her leather gloves back on, Brandy turned toward the car door.

"This is Odile, my personal secretary," the formidable Mrs. Demaine had said just a few days earlier, introducing Odile to Brandy. Brandy's attitude toward Mrs. Demaine, Odile, and everything around her in the mansion had been one of respectful attention. But when Mrs. Demaine had left them alone together, Brandy gave Odile the quickest once-over. A cat-that-swallowed-the-canary expression crossed her face, and was gone.

Odile reached out her hand then, and so did Brandy.

"So you've worked here a long time?" said Brandy, raising an eyebrow ever so slightly.

Mrs. Demaine had said nothing about how long Odile had worked there.

Odile was left to show Brandy around the place. It was huge and airy with giant windows everywhere, kitted sparsely but very expensively with the finest furnishings and art, of course. Brandy said nothing, but nodded from time to time as Odile showed her about.

Then, suddenly: "So, tell me something. The uniforms around here—including mine—pretty hot, eh?" She put her hands on her hips, twisting to the right and left, comically imitating the gesture some 1950s model would make and winking. "She's not expecting to bang us all, is she? Does she design them herself?"

People did not usually talk this way about Mrs. Demaine, even behind her back. "She does indeed," said Odile, looking downward, "and no she does not."

Brandy raised her eyebrows at Odile, who seemed suddenly to realize the unintentionally comic ambiguity of her own answer. She corrected herself. "That is, she does design the uniforms, with the help of an outfitter, and no, she most definitely does not intend to 'bang' anyone, as you said."

Brandy laughed. She turned around, winked over her shoulder, and sashayed off, the line of her bum zipper twitching back and forth provocatively.

Then, a day later, Odile had entered the front hall of the mansion with a bundle of files held close to her chest to find Mrs. Demaine there. Brandy was standing before her, receiving her instructions for the day. When she stood to attention like that her ass jutted back just a wee bit more than seemed necessary.

Was it because she knew Odile was behind her?

Mrs. Demaine finished and left, and Brandy turned. "Oh," she said, seeming to be surprised by Odile's presence, "it's you. I like your skirt." She gave Odile a proprietary smile, as if confident the skirt had been worn for herself.

Odile's voice was cool. "Thank you." It was one of her best skirts: long and tight, made of thick, dark green leather, buttoning up the side.

Brandy smiled a little more. "I think we both look good in leather, don't you? But wearing a whole suit of it can be uncomfortable. It can be so hot and sticky inside." Brandy looked down at Odile's skirt. "I always prefer wearing pants. But I like a girl in skirts. It makes me feel in control. You know?" She stepped forward and put her leather-gloved hand ever so lightly on Odile's hip, just where the large buttons held her skirt tightly closed. Odile clutched the files to her chest more tightly and glanced down at Brandy's pants, trying not to stare at the flap.

It bulged just a little. Brandy was lean, but her lower tummy was not perfectly so. Ah, that bit of a strain on the pants always took Odile's breath away. The flap clearly had no functional purpose, even though it obviously worked. What could Mrs. Demaine have been thinking? Odile knew her to be above suspicion when it came to matters of sexual interference with the servants. But was there some suppressed fantasy here, some subterranean and voyeuristic fetish of the subordinates rutting away...

"I don't know what she expects me to do with this flap," said Brandy, as if reading Odile's mind. "It doesn't really make any sense unless one has a dick, does it? Not that there'd be any room in here for that. You know, a girl, while waiting idly at the wheel in a parking lot could..." her hand moved slightly in that direction and a sly smile played about her lips.

Odile looked sideways out the window and interrupted with a sudden, forced brightness: "So. Are all your instructions for the day clear to you?"

"Yeah," said Brandy slowly, eyeing Odile in a knowing manner. "I know what to do."

"Well then," Odile said, bustling about with the files, which had nearly slipped out of her grasp, "I guess you should do it?" She hurried away, and was not sure, but thought she could just hear Brandy faintly laughing to herself.

Now Odile stared out the window, watching the retreating backside of the Silver Ghost as Brandy drove away. The egg came to a boil in the little pot. Odile turned the heat off and put the lid on.

Near the hot plate was an oversized, red plastic egg ticking away: a timer. Odile picked it up, wound and set it, and held it meditatively before her face. Along the circumference were marked the minutes.

The phone rang again and Odile answered it, staring into space. After a brief conversation, she hung up.

Taiwan: where Odile had helped Mrs. Demaine move some jobs out of Europe—to a place that had no unions. To a place where labor was cheap and people even more desperate than they were here.

Market forces. Survival of the fittest.

"Reality."

No, she thought, *she doesn't bang us.* Not in the way Brandy thought, anyway.

She had always hoped for better for herself. How did she end up here doing what she did not believe in?

The plastic egg ticked on. Suddenly, it rang, vibrating with a violent intensity. The real egg was ready.

The next day. Brandy breezed through the open door of Odile's office. She glanced down at the book on Odile's desk. "Karl Marx? *The Economic and Philosophical Manuscripts?*" She picked the book up, smiling. "Heavy stuff, Odile..."

It was the first time she had said Odile's name.

Brandy flipped through the book and put it down.

"You've come about the receipts for those auto parts?" asked Odile.

"Does she," nodding in the general direction of Mrs. Demaine's office, "know you read this stuff?"

"Probably not, but I don't give a shit."

"I'll bet you're smart enough not to let her see it, though."

With one arm dangling casually from her side she stepped forward and seized Odile with the other arm around the waist. "Oh you rebel you," Brandy said mockingly. She pressed her lips to Odile's and bent her backward like a bow and kissed her, the leather of Brandy's pants creaking as their bellies pressed together. Odile's hands fluttered out in apparent confusion. One braced her by the edge of the desk and the other lit upon the younger woman's shoulders and pressed back.

Brandy released her and stepped back, smiling.

"You'd love to get into my pants, wouldn't you, Odile? I like you."

"You like being in charge."

"Yes."

"Would you like to take charge of me?"

"Perhaps. Some time. Not now."

"You like toying with me. Tormenting me."

"Yes."

Odile trembled a little and brushed a strand of hair from her face. "You are young enough, I suppose, to feel you have a right to anything."

"I have a right to you."

"Do you?"

"Oh yes. And you'd like to say no, just to prove you can, but you can't."

"Fuck you!"

"Oh yes. You certainly will. This hot young thing? How can you resist?" Brandy ran her leather-gloved hand lightly through Odile's hair around her ear. Involuntarily, Odile tilted her head and shoulder toward Brandy, closed her eyes and murmured slightly. Brandy spoke close to her other ear.

"I kind of like you older chicks. I think it's because you've been around the block a few times and know how to please a girl."

"Fucking arrogant little bitch," said Odile, her eyes still closed.

"Yes. And it's more important to you now to please someone, isn't it?"

She smiled, turned and left.

Next day:

Brandy walked into Odile's office again. They were supposed to discuss the scheduling of some important visitors from a trade delegation who would need Brandy to drive them.

"Close the door please," said Odile, glancing up from her desk, looking a little faint.

Brandy gave her an arch look, and took a step or two back toward the door, her face still looking at Odile over her shoulder. She closed and locked the door.

"I can't wait any more," said Odile. She stood up, clutching her hands before her. "I know I'm risking making a complete idiot of myself, but I'm yours."

Brandy tilted her face down just a little, smiling. She stepped forward with her hands crossed over her chest, then raised a gloved hand to Odile's hair and toyed with it lightly. "You certainly work fast, don't you?"

"Oh Ma'am," Odile said, "it would be an honor. May I? Still hot and sticky in there? Let's find out. Let's visit where Miss Pussy lives. I want to please her."

Brandy laughed. "Eager to please, are you? I have to drive soon. Look at these pants, Odile. Do you think these are pants I can quickly get out of and then back into before I have to…"

"May I? May I please?" she said, gesturing to the inviting flap.

Brandy smiled wryly, put her hands on her hips. "Well, all right. Since you've been so respectful. But we don't have long…"

Odile bent forward and her fingers flew swiftly to work. One zipper went down, then the other. She quickly opened the buttons and the flap sprung open, revealing black panties with words on the middle as if on a traffic sign:

NO EXIT.

"Like my panties? Just a little chauffeuse's joke."

"Oh my love, they're adorable. Let me get my fingers in them. Ooh! You're hairless. I do so like that. So clean and smooth. Mmmm…"

Brandy's face was tilted back to the ceiling. Her eyes popped open in sudden astonishment. Odile's fingers were long and thin and skillful, and she set to work as one knowing exactly what to do.

"Oh! Odile, I…wait, I…"

"Feel nice?"

"Oh, yes."

"Like my fingers in there?"

"Oh! Yes… Oh, Odile, how are you doing that?…"

"I play the violin. It's good training…"

"Is it ever!" she gushed, bending at the knees a little. She took her hands off her hips and staggered back a couple of steps, bum bumping up against Odile's desk. She put her hands there for support. "Unh!"

"I can play the pussy too."

"Unhh!"

"Shhh, Mistress, not so loud please."

"Oh!"

"I can play any girl, especially the silly young ones who think they know everything."

"I'm sorry, I can't hear anything. I'm on cloud nine."

Odile continued to busy her fingers about Brandy's labia and clit, lightly humming a little tune.

Brandy trembled. "Odile, I'm going to spurt! My pants will get wet."

"I figured you for an ejaculator..."

"Unh..."

"I just knew you were a pants wetter..."

"Oh..."

"You smooth-cunted bitch, you leather-sheathed animal..."

"Nnnngh..."

Odile turned from her for a moment toward the desk and the timing egg. She grasped it and wound it up. It began to tick loudly. She slathered it in lubricant she had handy just inside the desk drawer. Brandy leaned against the desk still, gasping, eyes closed in helpless ecstasy.

"I know a little chicken who's going to lay an egg for me. Want to lay an egg, little chicken?

"Odile?"

"Get a load of this, honey." Odile slowly but firmly pushed the big ticking egg up her oozing quim.

"Huh? Oh! What the fuck! Odile, oh god, that feels good... What the...?" Her cunt seized the egg involuntarily in an iron grip. In ecstasy and confusion, Brandy began to babble incoherently.

"Now," said Odile, "let's just slip a sanitary pad in there under your panties—a nice thick one—to keep your pants dry. We don't want your pants wet for when the boss comes."

"Huh?"

"Mrs. Demaine will be here any minute. We are to look over some accounts together. And you know how prompt she is. To the very minute," she said glancing at her watch, "the very minute."

Odile wedged the pad, which came from the same drawer as the lubricant, into Brandy's panties. Then she let the tight little panties slip back into place.

Brandy was breathing heavily.

"I always looked a little nervous in your presence, didn't I?" said Odile. "But it wasn't fear. It wasn't some feeling of unworthiness. It was sheer excitement. Sheer anticipation of what I was going to do with you. And you had no idea."

Faintly, a ticking sound could be heard coming from Brandy's cunt.

She stared at Odile in confusion, a bead of sweat on her forehead, one eye half-closed in the throes of sexual excitement. Odile pushed at the egg from outside Brandy's panties, and Brandy's cunt tensed about it, pushing it forward again. Odile pressed it back in, and they both went back and forth like this awhile.

"Sweet little helpless pussy," cooed Odile.

"Oh my god. Odile, don't stop. You have to bring me off."

"I don't have to do anything, sweetie," Odile said, patting her on the cheek. "I'm in charge." She looked at her watch. "My estimate is, it will take ten minutes to cook that egg."

Brandy stood knock-kneed like a little girl trying not to pee herself. "Odile? What did you put in me? What's it doing? I can f-feel it ticking or something."

"I've given you a clockwork cunt, my dear. As long as you are satisfied to be a piece of the machinery, you may as well play the role to the hilt."

"P-piece of the machinery?"

"You drive, but you don't go anywhere. Not of your own volition. Not in your own car. Is that freedom? Am I free in this office, which doesn't belong to me, which is in someone else's house, where I help the boss scheme to take other people's livelihood? Do you think we can find a way, Brandy? A way together?" It was the first time she had spoken her name to her.

Brandy stared at her, slightly cross-eyed, and said "I can't talk political philosophy right now, love."

"She owns us, you know. Wouldn't you like not to be owned, Brandy? Except, perhaps, by an equal? Like me? Like I'm owning you now?"

Odile pushed her hand again against Brandy's pantied pubis, pushing the egg deeper than before.

Brandy gasped.

"Do you think of yourself as a top, Brandy? With your attitude and your leather uniform? I don't think so. I just let you think that. Now you've got an egg timer up your cooter and you're helpless with pleasure, aren't you sweetie?"

"Oh yes..."

"Fresh and young and confident, proudly beginning your life of servitude in your little uniform. Do you know what my fantasy is, Brandy? My fantasy is to fuck you right in front of our boss. To show her I own you, she doesn't. My fantasy is to make you pregnant with the egg of revolution. Does that make any sense to you girl?"

"Oh god! You're not going to make me come right in front of her..."

"Relax, hon. We'll keep our jobs for now. Just wrap your lips around this, cutie," Odile said, knocking lightly between Brandy's legs. "This thing really shakes when it goes off. Like a vibrator."

"Huh? Wh-when?"

"Um..." Odile rolled her eyes in thoughtful, mock innocence.

"I'm not sure. I forgot what I set it at. I suppose it could be any moment. Or as long as an hour from now. But when it does go off—BAM! Right to the moon."

Brandy groaned.

"All that is solid, melts into orgasm. I've invaded your uniform, girl, and planted the flag, the red flag, the red egg, the wind of revolution blows up your..."

There was a knock on the door. "Odile? Why is your door locked?"

It was Mrs. Demaine.

Brandy shot a desperate, *help-rescue-me* look into Odile's face. Calmly, Odile put a finger to her lips and began to zip up Brandy's pants and button them, egg still stuffed in her cunt.

Brandy gasped, astonished.

"Odile? Are you ready?" asked Mrs. Demaine through the door.

Odile opened the door. "My apologies, ma'am. I must have locked it by accident. I was just going over with Brandy the arrangements for tomorrow."

Mrs. Demaine bustled in with a thick folder of documents in her arms. She seemed unconcerned with the excuses. "Oh. Hello, Brandy."

Brandy nodded a sweaty, nervous smile, just barely managing to keep her lips from trembling. Still leaning against the desk, she crossed her arms across her chest, trying desperately to give off an air of nonchalance.

"Relax, Brandy, sit down. Odile and I won't be but a moment."

"No thank you, ma'am, I'd rather stand."

Mrs. Demaine bent over Odile's desk, back turned, and laid out some papers. Brandy tottered slightly bowlegged to the open door and gingerly stepped into the hallway. "Um, I'm afraid I simply must get off now. I mean, be off."

She stepped gingerly into the hall and closed the door behind her. A moment later, a ringing sound came faintly through the door and something like a deep, stifled groan.

"What's that?" said Mrs. Demaine, blinking. "Is that Brandy?"

"No, ma'am. Just the wind."

TWO WOMEN HAVING SEX

Elna Holst

I'd like to tell you the story of two women having sex. It has to be short; I don't have much time. Let's keep it simple.

One could be Anna, princess of the palindromes. She could be anyone, from anywhere. Let's just say she's from around here.

The other is Ellen, the love interest. She's not terribly impressed by the title. Tough.

Now, we need a location for the pair to strike their chord. We'll be up-to-date and egalitarian and say: midpoint from here to there. Though the trains don't stop midpoint. Cars, bikes, cross-country skiing? Anna is more pragmatic: the town of M——. An invitation drops into Ellen's disordered mailbox. A letter of assignation. Oh, come.

(Ellen goes off on a tangent. She liked the idea of snow.) A date is set, tickets are booked. Not too far into the future. People have their needs.

Fortunately, Ellen's job is flexible. She is basically her own boss. And oh can she be bossy... But not today. Anna's a mature student, which means, for the present, she has to live Here. Fine, though inconvenient, when all her wet dreams are centered around There. No, not *there*, you dirty. Well all right. There too.

Bright and early one morning, when the sun is just a hint of pink beyond the high-rises in the fairly large (though globally inconsequential) city of There, Ellen's alarm goes off, telling her: *Bag by the door. Go to train station. Ticket in your inside pocket—put jacket on!* Ellen is not a morning person. She needs her instructions, spelled out.

She does remember, however, to don a clean pair of slacks. Go through the toothbrush and toothpaste thing. Touch some wax to the tips of her 'do.

Already, through the haze, anticipation is building up within her. As she hoists the overnight bag onto her shoulder, fumbling with the keys to lock the front door, she imagines Anna, waking up leisurely, all golden fuzz and honeyed limbs. The sun is pushing through a convenient gap in the curtains, fingering an erect nipple here, the hopelessly soft spot behind an ear there. Ellen touches her own spot. The one behind the ear.

At the train station, she picks up breakfast: pancakes, box of raisins, coffee—double black. She never skips breakfast. There have to be rules.

In Here, Anna sheaths those nipples in a cotton bra. She wears black, usually, but has chosen off-white for the occasion. She knows Ellen appreciates the see-through effect. Gathering her things, she rakes up some notes, at random, for something to read on the ride. She opens the fridge, wrinkles her nose in distaste, and closes it again. No breakfast for Anna, the bender of rules.

Well, maybe a cup of Earl Grey on board. Extra sugar. She could stomach that.

Ellen's train has the farthest to go, by half an hour or so. She's not what you would call of a numerical mind. All she knows is she will be there on time, if it pleaseth, and so forth. It's on her ticket: *09:42*. A quarter to ten, she called it, in her reply. *See u. xx.*

The train pulses along the tracks, slowly, grindingly, bringing her up to the main event. She is throbbing in her seat, her palms tickling with imagined touch. But let's not overindulge in wanton fantasies. We are heading, after all, for the Real Deal.

At her station, Anna is passing the time by synchronizing her wristwatch with the clock on her phone. She does those kinds of things. A keeper of times. Her ticket says *09:46*. Close enough.

Although she's a sucker for the simultaneous, once in a blue moon—such a thrill.

Her train pulls in with half a minute's delay. She tries (fails) not to frown at the annoyingly complacent ticket inspector. They'll catch up.

At this point in our narrative, you might be wondering where, specifically, the tryst is to take place? Bathroom stall, unlikely nook or cranny, shielded by shrubbery in a public park? The town of M— is surely too diminutive for a sizeable municipal plantation? Besides, it's March, north of most of you, though south of the Arctic, to be sure. *We're too old for that,* types Ellen—come summer, though, Anna will have proved her wrong. Oh come summer... Where were we? Ellen: *I've booked a room.*

Pricey, says Anna (student, remember).

My treat.

Ellen's got her mind on some gourmet nosh in the restaurant, afterward. If there's time.

The train shudders to a halt between stations. Anna feels a pinch of panic, recalling a five-hour delay, not too long ago. Ruined dinner, but...

"We are waiting to be passed by an oncoming train," the tannoy bleats. "This will not affect our schedule."

She sits back in her seat, texts: *False alarm.*

You didn't imagine there was no form of communication, did you? Romantic as the notion may be, they are not two sailboats, meeting in the night. Just two ordinary women (about to have sex).

Ellen sends a short vid of her fingers, drumming against the table, on her northbound journey.

Anna titters, and then glances sideways at her fellow passengers. Returns a: *Hush.*

Ellen brings out a book. One hour to go.

But we can't very well wait an hour, can we? Cut to: firs flitting by; cut to: village of this and that; cut to: Anna gets off the train. Ellen is already there, reaching for her rucksack to hang over her other shoulder—ever the gentlewoman. Also, it gives Anna some leeway with her cane (yes, there's a cane at this point, mild cerebral palsy, no mental deficiency, don't look so surprised). See what we did there? The beauty of cuts.

"Where to, good woman?"

"*Das Stadthotel.*"

No, they're not German, or turn-of-a-bygone-century. They just talk like that.

As they link hands, there's a moment thick with electricity. They laugh, almost shyly, and Ellen pulls along, leading the way. Neither of them has ever had a reason to visit M——, but it's puny (did I mention that?), and as it happens, the hotel in question is right on the other side of the tracks.

On the way, Ellen slips the check-in instructions into the pocket of Anna's coat. "I booked it in your name, but don't worry, it's all been paid. Free minibar."

Ellen is not a fan of check-in situations. Anna kisses the tip of her nose.

"One of these days…"

They arrive at the lobby of the out-of-place, moderately large building at 10:01. Check-in opens at ten. Lucky them.

"One night only?" the woman behind the counter inquires, looking over the rim of her hot-pink, leopard-print reading glasses.

"One night," Anna smiles. "Passing through."

Ellen nods her head vigorously half a step behind her,

wobbling with the sudden swing of their scanty luggage, putting on her most businesslike, innocent-looking mien. The leopard-prints waver doubtfully between them, then turn back to the not-so-flat computer screen.

"All right then," the woman sighs, handing over the requisite brightly colored folders, key cards, receipt. "I hope you'll find the room nice and comfortable. Just give me a ring if you need anything."

Anna thanks her. Says something commonplace. Maybe even compliments M—— a little. She's suave that way.

In the elevator, Ellen pins her to the wall. This is cliché, but she's well on desperate. She sticks her nose down the open neck of Anna's shirt, breathing in the smell of her, like coke. She doesn't say *I've missed you*. No need.

"Now there's a way to treat a person with a cane," Anna chides, cheeks red, eyes glittering.

"Mm," Ellen agrees, digging in deeper, "you can treat me to your cane."

She tugs at the shirt, pulling the lapels down and to the side so that she can press her lips to the very tops of Anna's breasts. Anna shivers. The doors of the lift ping open. Ellen spins around, covering her rumpled partner-in-crime with her back. Of course, there's no one there.

"Partner-in-crime? Really?" says Anna, scanning the numbers along the corridor for their room.

Fine. Just partner, then.

"I like partner-in-life," Anna suggests, pushing the key card into the lock of the door to the right. Ellen flushes with delight.

The door clicks open. Here we go.

Bags are dropped to the floor. The cane is summarily discarded in the easy chair by the window. Ellen sits on the queen-size bed and Anna sits on her lap, on cue, wrapping her slim, trim legs around her, letting her chosen partner-in-life finish what was so rudely interrupted by the opening of elevator doors. Ellen unbuttons her shirt. Pushes the cute but in-the-way off-white bra out of the way. Fills her hands with soft, rosy treasure. Or better yet—tits.

Anna holds onto Ellen's shoulders, close to purring, as her lover licks and sucks, fondles and squeezes, forgetting all about plot, structure, grammar rules and anagrams. Who needs anagrams, for that matter, when you have kilograms of Anna at your disposal?

"Kilograms?"

Ellen comes up for a breather, her hair pointing directions to all over the place. Her face is brimming with bliss.

"Pounds and pounds," she nods, and weighs the palindrome in her arms.

Anna is already unbearably wet. Ellen should know this. But she is taking her sweet time.

"Could we...?" Anna indicates the length and width of the bed. Ellen helps her out of the constraints of her crumpled shirt.

"Why not? While we're at it."

And into bed they tumble, naked, skipping out on the preliminaries (you know the drill). Ellen pulls Anna close. Anna pulls Ellen closer, her legs parting to accommodate Ellen's thigh. A tremor runs through them both as Anna's wetness slips along Ellen's skin. Their pubic bones press together, heat prickling and flashing wherever body parts meet in joint, frustrating desire. Anna nibbles at Ellen's ear, finding the spot, there, here, scratching it with her teeth, muttering: "I'm going to die if you don't fuck me soon."

Ellen is only too happy to comply. Lifting Anna's bottom up from off the mattress, she plunges two fingers into her, heading right for the nubbly spot of her vaginal wall. Anna's head falls back with a guttural "Yes," her body arching like the old round-stone bridge across the river of the town of M—— (or is it Here?) to meet her thrust, to take her even deeper. Arousal drips from Ellen onto the crisp Egyptian cotton of the hotel's bedsheets, as she finds her rhythm, that rhythm that has her lean-limbed love writhing and gurgling with *joie de vivre. Comme il faut.* She bends her head to French kiss Anna's puffy parts, keeping her fingers pushing and slipping, stressing and dipping, punctuating her message with the silky, insistent sweeps of her tongue.

"Oh fuck!" Anna eloquently enjoinders, and Ellen revs it up a notch, increasing her pressure, tripping up the speed, her free hand finding Anna's to stroke the tingling, sensitive point of her racing pulse with her thumb, and Anna is coming, coming as surely as the train from Here to There, roaring down the rails like a *tour de force*, like a stutter of hand-holding exclamation marks, again, again, again, the bridge tensing and crumbling, the river flowing with the spring flood, Ellen's fingers refusing derailment, sucked, as it were, into an airtight lock.

Anna hits the mattress orgasming, tangling with the source of her enjoyment. The source buffets her with her head. They disentangle, for an instant, to make heads and tails of the bed again.

Ellen props herself up on a pillow, her cunt swelling with self-conceited pride at the sight of Anna's (temporarily) sated glow. She looks like...

"Stop! No more poetry, for the moment, please—though you certainly have a way with French." Anna closes in, her fingers trailing down Ellen's abdomen. Ellen's breath catches.

"So..." Anna lifts an eyebrow, fingertips dawdling along the edge of Ellen's pubic hair. "What was it you were saying earlier? Something about my cane?"

In the wee hours of the night, they empty the contents of the minibar onto the bed. We'll call it a feast.

"I'm sorry about the restaurant closing and all," Anna offers, crunching on ridiculously salty mini-pretzels, not, to be frank, looking all that sorry. She does on the other hand look good enough to eat. Hours of lovemaking will do that to you.

Ellen takes another swig of her half-emptied Carlsberg.

"Don't." Anna breaks open a chocolate bar, scrambling to find the remote for the ceiling-mounted TV in the corner.

"What?"

"There is not a jot of energy left in me. Not a gram, you hear? I'm emptied out, dried up, a complete desert in between rain periods. It's too late for this. Also, I need my news fix. You'll just have to wait."

Ellen puts the bottle down on the nightstand. Takes a bite of the chocolate Anna holds out to her as a distraction. The TV flickers to life.

With a contented sigh, Anna leans back against the head-board. She smooths the duvet out over them both. Ellen hands the candy bar back to her.

"All comfy?" she queries, a distinct glint in her eyes, and sure enough, seconds later she is under the covers, burrowing into a little nest just, as it happens, between the thighs of her news-watching nubile. The would-be nubile protests.

"I feel more like a geriatric wing dropout, you know, and you better stop that, what will the readers…"

Ellen's head comes up to meet Anna's gaze, haloed by tousled sheets.

"You can see the screen from there, can't you?"

Anna's eyes flit over to the flurry of images and text. She has put it on mute, because it's three o'clock in the morning, and people need their rest.

Some people.

Ellen looks at her earnestly.

"You really want me to stop?"

Anna makes a face. Shakes her head. Ellen dips down to lick some stray grains of salt from Anna's strained, sweat-streaked midriff. A quiver ripples over the hypersensitized flesh. Anna groans. Opens her legs a touch wider. Her sex is luscious, warm and inviting. Ellen puts her face up close, her exhalations enough to make a little moisture ooze out from between those kiss-stung nether lips.

"I could stop," she says, enunciating her words carefully, struggling for a moment's sobriety. "Just tell me to stop."

Anna reaches over to the pile of loot from the minibar. She tears open another bar of chocolate, splitting off a healthy chunk. Her eyes locked on to Ellen's, she parts herself with the fingers of her left hand and nudges the piece of sticky sweetness in between her folds.

"You could stop," Anna allows, melting down the headboard as quickly as the chocolate. "But it would stain."

Ellen would never let good foodstuff go to waste. She is much too much of an environmentalist. Chocoholic. Sex addict. Take your pick. (Also, she hates to leave a mess for the cleaners. Which Anna knows fine well.)

INK AND CANVAS

Geonn Cannon

I tensed when the nib touched my shoulder, cold ink and even colder steel against skin still supple from my bath. "Okay?" Lina whispered. I nodded; I wasn't allowed to speak while she was writing. I was kneeling on the bed with my feet under me. The towel was still around my waist, but I was otherwise naked. Lina sat behind me on the bed. She was still fully dressed in the suit she'd worn to work, missing only the blazer to show off her sleeveless silk blouse. She brought the stylus back to my shoulder and drew an arc. I suppressed a shudder and faced forward. My eyes closed, my lips tight, as I kept track of the words she was writing.

Livid with its strong lines, peaks and valleys.

Extraordinary, a long word that stretched across my shoulder blade, and then brought her back through the word to cross the X, the T, and dot the I.

Lyrical with its ups and downs increased by making the letters tall and slanted.

The movement of the sharp stylus tip across my skin made

me shudder. The ink was cool and I could feel it drying when Lina moved on to the next word.

Supple.

Possession.

Sydney.

I smiled when she wrote my name, turning my head to acknowledge without saying anything. Lina shifted on the mattress. She had been using one arm to prop herself up, but she moved it to my hip. She wrote *beach*, *sensual*, *tongue*, *thigh*, and my breathing increased as each word became more suggestive. Lina wrote small, but the words still crowded one quadrant of my back. She finished with a cursive—*fini*—and put the stylus down. She leaned close, her lips almost touching my skin, and blew across the words she'd written to dry the ink faster. Her hand slid along my hip, under the towel, and stroked the inside of my thigh.

I leaned back against her and said, "Thank you, Ma'am."

"You're very welcome." She kissed my neck and accepted my weight. She ran her writing hand over my other hip, over my stomach, and cupped my breast. The skin was still tender where she had written today's words. I had another list on my other shoulder, faded by the bath but still legible. *Rosemary* and *bright* and *shallots* and *champagne*, these written in an arc that followed the line of my shoulder up to my neck. More words, faded even further, marched down the length of my spine: *sweet*, *lie*, *caress*, *cerulean*, *difference*, *labia*, *dew*, *harken*. I remembered them all even though I had never seen them. I'd only felt them being written.

None of the words would be visible when I dressed for work in the morning; my Lady would choose an outfit that covered them all well. We weren't embarrassed by the ritual. It was simply something that belonged to only us.

It started not long after we first became a couple. Lina discovered my submissive personality and began exploring her

Dominant side. The first few weeks, all of her demands were formed inquisitively. "Would you like it if I laid out your clothes for work?" or "What if I asked you not to speak for an entire evening?" I would always reply with, "If it makes you happy, my love." She gave me the option and I handed it back to her with my head bowed. She became my Mistress, and I was simply hers. Her property, her most treasured possession. Sometimes she called me *darling,* sometimes *pet.* My favorite was *toy,* because I *am* her toy. She could play with me whenever she wanted, however she wanted.

The first time she wrote on me was at an art auction. She'd never purchased anything in the time I'd known her, but she liked to see the lots, to see a spirited competition between bidders, and to spend an hour or two in such exquisite company. I had never been to one, but I was quickly enamored by it. Everyone looked like refugees from another time, a more gilded age. The auctioneer wore white gloves and spoke with a sharp New England accent, all stiff jaw and proper enunciation. I wore a black gown that my Lady had chosen for me, and she was dressed in a black pinstripe suit with a lacy, low-cut top.

We watched as priceless artifacts were placed next to the auctioneer's podium and listened as he detailed each one's provenance and history. The pieces were contemporary and all came with names I'd never heard of—Adrian Ghenie, Lucio Fontana, Yves Klein—along with artists whose names I recognized—Warhol and Lichtenstein and Elizabeth Peyton.

Midway through the show, my Lady reached over and used her fingers to widen the slit on the side of my gown. She exposed my upper thigh, the lacy top of my stockings. My cheeks reddened at the thought of the man on my left seeing what she had done, but I didn't dare complain. I bit my lip and looked toward the front of the room. She had been taking notes on each item, but she moved the pen and pressed the tip against my thigh. The first letter was large and made of two smooth curves that ended with an upward tick. It was followed by a curvy, upright line that looked like a crowbar. Another arch, and then a curl like a pig's tail.

MINE.

A feeling of happiness spread through my chest. I covered her hand, which she had flattened over the marking. The warmth and weight of her hand pressing against the word seemed to burn it into my skin. Even all these years later, I could still feel the sharp scroll of that pen as it moved over my sensitive flesh and left a black mark in its wake.

That night, when she scrubbed away the mark in our bath, I asked if she would give me a tattoo. The act of letting her mark me that way was such a turn-on, I could only imagine how it would feel to have something etched into my skin for her. But she said no. "I don't want to commit to anything permanent. I would like to keep you as my blank canvas."

There currently wasn't any ink on my front, but sometimes she drew pictures on my thighs. A sparrow, a flower. Sometimes she would write her name in a belt around my waist, linking the letters in a chain I could feel all day even though it was just ink. I loved having her words on me. I loved wearing them and felt sad when they finally faded. But if they were tattoos, I would have been covered from knee to collar with my Lady's thoughts, her whispers, her creations. As much as I wanted that, I wanted even more to see what else she could come up with.

The first few words were written with whatever pen happened to be convenient. She wrote in red, in blue, in black, in purple. After a few months, when we both understood just how special this ceremony was, I gifted her with a beautiful wooden box with solid brass hardware. When she got home from work she found me seated on the divan with it on my lap. My hands were folded over the ornate carving on its lid. I held it out to her, looking up through my lashes.

"For you, my Lady."

She took it from me and thumbed open the latch. Inside she found the calligraphy set. There were three styluses, each hand-carved from different kinds of wood for a variety of weight. It had six interchangeable nibs, sharp and elegantly curved to give her a choice of thickness in her lines. It came with a small jar of black ink, and Lina brushed her fingers over the glass with a look of wonder. She lifted the bottle and smiled at me.

"Go to the bedroom and undress."

That night I'd gotten my first installment of words. Lina started with *beautiful, gorgeous, lovely, submit.* She moved on to harsher words like *slut* and *whore,* but she drew them with such care and elegance that I felt they were terms of endearment in this context. She could have written anything on me with that stylus and it would have felt like the highest of compliments. She also wrote her full name—*LINA ROSE RYAN*—across my forehead and then kissed the ink.

"I love my gift, Sydney. Thank you."

I smiled at the memory. The wooden box was on the night-stand, but the stylus was on the mattress next to me. I wasn't allowed to touch it unless instructed, but sometimes I wondered what I would write on Lina's body if she gave me the chance. Dominant, of course. Grand. Elegant. Love. I closed my eyes and let my legs fall apart. My Lady dragged her hand up the inside of my thigh and placed her hand on the mattress between my legs. I sank down until my pussy was against her wrist. She bowed down and kissed my lips, her other hand still playing with my breast as I rolled my hips. First up, along the length of her arm, then back down, digging my heels into the mattress, my toes curled. I moved my hands back to grip her legs for leverage.

"My Lady," I whispered, "please..."

She moved her hand up so that her fingers were against me, the two in the center stroking along my folds before easing them apart. I raised my head and Lina made me stretch to find her mouth. My lips were trembling when they met hers, and she moved her hand from my breast to cradle my head. I pushed myself up so I was lying more completely on her lap as she twisted her fingers inside of me.

When we broke the kiss, I lay back down across her lap. I kept my eyes open to watch my Lady, her black hair pinned back, her lips ruby red, her brown-black eyes running up and down the length of my body to watch how I reacted to her touch. I trembled and whimpered; my toes curled and my hands clutched at her skirt.

"Come for me, darling," Lina whispered.

I arched my back and did as she commanded. She dragged her fingers from me and used them to tease the sensitive spots of my clit and my folds before dragging her nails over my mound. I shivered and closed my eyes as I settled back onto her lap. I stretched my legs out straight and sighed.

"Thank you, my Lady."

"You are more than welcome, woman of mine." She smiled and bent down to kiss my lips, dragging her tongue across them as her hand continued to roam over my body.

When I was able, I sat up and helped Lina out of her clothes. Each item was carefully folded and placed into the hamper, where it would stay until I took it to the dry cleaner. When my Lady was nude, she spread her legs and I knelt between them. She guided my head down and I used my tongue on her. I drew words of my own with the tip of my tongue: *gracious*, *kind*, *adoration*, *queen*, *tight*, *wet*. She pushed her hands through my hair as I made her writhe.

I wrapped my arms around her legs so I could flatten my hands on her stomach. I applied gentle pressure and she took my hint, lying down as she brought her feet up to rest them on my back. Her gasps and whimpers were like music to me; I had taken away her words, they were burnt on my skin, and now all she had left were the moans that I could elicit with my tongue and lips. My Lady's fingers curled when I pushed her to orgasm, pulling my hair as she cried out. Her shoulders lifted off the bed for the duration of her climax, lowering only when her entire body went limp.

"Is my Lady satisfied?"

"Yes," she sighed. "Your Lady is very satisfied. You were a very good toy tonight."

I smiled and crawled up her body. I lay on top of her, my head on her chest as she enclosed me in an embrace. She kissed the top of my head and I craned my neck to find her lips. She flickered her tongue against my mouth and I laughed quietly before returning the gesture. She squirmed away from me and I sat up.

"Put away the kit, please."

"Yes, Ma'am." I gathered the stylus and returned it to the box. After making sure the inkwell was properly stoppered, I closed the lid and thumbed the latch back in place. While I was putting it away, Lina repositioned her head on the pillows and smoothed out the blanket and sheet. I crawled in next to her and placed my head on her chest.

"Pleasant dreams, Lina," I whispered.

She brushed a strand of hair away from my face. "Good night, Sydney."

I sighed blissfully, contented, and let the sound of her breathing serenade me to sleep.

I woke at 5:13. It was free time, so I slipped from our bed and walked on the balls of my feet to the bathroom down the hall. I did my business, then went through my exercises. When I was finished, I took a shower. Afterward I wrapped a towel around my waist and went to the full-length mirror on the back of the bathroom door. I twisted so I could examine my Lady's work. The newest ink was a bit faded; perhaps I shouldn't have showered so soon after getting it done. She would be annoyed and I would likely face punishment. I felt a thrill at the possibility, but

I pushed it out of my mind to finish getting ready.

The few friends and acquaintances who knew details of our relationship found it unusual, to be kind. A few assumed that she hit me or that our physical relationship consisted solely of her whipping or spanking me. Without getting into details, I assured them that they had no reason to be concerned. Yes, she had spanked me. She'd choked me, tied me up, punished me for being naughty or breaking the rules. But it wasn't about violence or inflicting pain. I couldn't explain it to them without getting into details far too intimate to share with friends, but I did my best to ease their worries.

I knelt in front of the dresser and opened the bottom drawer, where all of my clothes were neatly folded. My Lady's outfits took up the majority of the closet space. Today's outfit was on top, blouse and skirt folded with the underwear and stockings inside. I dressed myself quickly, covering with silk the words my Lady had added to her lexicon the night before. I could almost feel the material brushing over the ink like a kiss.

Once dressed, I went back to the bed and crouched beside my Lady. She was sleeping peacefully, lips slightly parted and her hair hanging loose across her face. I brushed the strands back, ran the tip of my middle finger over her cheek and admired her for a long, quiet moment. Her fingers were curled beside the pillow, and I could see a smudge of ink on the inside of one finger. I wet the pad of my thumb and wiped it away. I woke Lina in the process and she gazed at me sleepily until I noticed.

"Good morning, my Lady," I whispered. "Did you sleep well?"

"As always. Yourself?"

"Splendidly." I smoothed her hair so she would look slightly more presentable when she faced herself in the mirror. "I have to go. Is there anything you need before I leave?"

Lina shook her head and kissed my hand. "Have a good day."

"Is that an order, my Lady?"

She grinned and lifted her head to kiss me properly. "Yes. I shall be very angry if you do not abide."

"Okay." I squeezed her shoulder and pulled the blanket back up over her.

I biked to the office, started a pot of coffee and took my station in front of my boss's office at three minutes to seven. I checked emails and messages, sorting them by priority and how I knew each one would be received. I was nearly finished when I heard the elevator ding. I transferred everything to my tablet and stood up with the computer held against my chest.

Lina came around the corner, attention focused on the phone in her hand. I smiled at the sight of her, all business and completely different from how I'd seen her just a few hours ago. She had been unguarded and vulnerable, a side she showed only to me. She glanced up at me as she passed my desk.

"Ms. West." She continued into her office without breaking pace. I pursued.

"Good morning, Ms. Ryan," I said. I placed the phone messages on her desk where she could sort them herself, then consulted the computer. "You have an eight-forty-five with Mr. Peabody, and lunch with Evelyn Jacobi from the Whitney. She emailed and said she would leave the restaurant up to you. I recommend Keens."

Lina nodded. "Very good. Call and make a reservation."

"Yes, Ma'am. Is there anything else you need?"

"Not at the moment."

I nodded. "Then I'll be at my desk." I started from the room, but Lina said my name before I reached the door. "Yes, Ms. Ryan?"

She held up a ballpoint pen. "This pen is out of ink."

"Oh, no." I walked back to the desk and took it from her. I flattened my palm and scribbled on the meaty part below my thumb. It left a thick black mark. "It seems to be working fine, Ma'am."

"Does it? My mistake."

Our fingers brushed when I handed the pen back to her. I knew exactly what I had done by purposefully marking myself. When we got home, I would be punished. My Lady smiled, and I had to fight the urge to smile back at her. I felt a tingle low in my gut as I envisioned what form my penalty would take. I didn't want to think about it, didn't want to begin the day with an itch I couldn't scratch, but her smile did things to me I couldn't control.

"Will there be anything else, Ma'am?"

"Not at the moment, Ms. West."

I nodded and turned on my heel, walking away from her. I ran my fingertips over the illicit ink on my palm, not daring to wash it off until I'd paid for the indiscretion. Lina would put me over her knee, or she would write horrible words on my arms and legs to make me pay for what I'd done. She would make me crawl. She might even make me sleep in the spare bedroom. I hoped it wouldn't be that one, but whatever punishment my Lady decided upon, I would accept it with grace and humility.

I could hardly wait to see what she would come up with.

COVERT AFFAIRS

V. Florian

The first time we meet, she pistol-whips me across the back of my head, bursting out of a dark corner of a safe house I thought was empty.

I'm angry when I come to again: she has me zip-tied to a chair, the back of my head hurts like fuck and it's been seven hours and four time zones since my last cup of coffee.

We're in Paris, or at least a suburb of Paris. I stare at her in the stark light of the bulb above our heads, the night just as stark black outside, but she's not looking at me. She is carefully cleaning a gun. We are in a dingy kitchen, strewn with dirty dishes from meals stuffed down by god only knows how many covert operatives who have made this their refuge for a few, uneasy hours. I'm not sure she knows I'm awake until she says: "I've another one in my lap, so don't try anything." Her accent is English. The rich kind, all sharp consonants and nasal vowels. I don't answer, and she looks up at me. She's blonde with sharp features, thinner than covert operatives usually are, pale to the point of being anemic. "I'm sorry. Do you speak English?"

"Why don't you get me the fuck out of this chair, and I'll tell you what languages I speak," I spit at her.

"You're CIA?"

"I could be with Santa Claus for all you should care, this ain't your safe house," I say. It's hard to tell when she's sitting down, but she looks a few inches taller than me. She is at least ten years older than me, though, and I have fifteen pounds of muscle on her. I could take her. "Who told you about this place?" I ask, as if we were making conversation. Behind my back, I'm carefully finding weak spots in my constraints.

"Someone owed me," she says, and starts putting her gun back together. "Someone didn't say you'd stop by though."

I could stay and make conversation, but I think better of it. While she's looking down at her work I make a break for it, overturning my chair and the table with it, splintering the back of that fragile old wooden chair and hightailing out of there. She takes a shot at me, but it's halfhearted, whistling through the air a fair few feet above my head.

I cut my zip-ties on a piece of broken rebar on an abandoned lot and spend the night rattling back and forth in the artificial light of the metro.

The second time we meet, she's all dressed up. I'm posing as a security officer at the American embassy in Ljubljana, and she makes me the second she gets in line for the metal detector. I ask her to get out of the line for additional questioning and sure, I'm being a bit rougher than strictly necessary when I pull her into the adjacent room. My head hurt for weeks after our first get-together. The sharp light and bare white walls in here make a stark contrast to the lush, luxurious rooms outside.

"What are you doing here?" I ask her. She doesn't answer. I have her pushed against a table, my gun between her ribs. "I'm going to pat you down and you're not going to move a single fucking muscle."

She won't have a gun on her. If she needs one she will have stashed it somewhere inside the embassy, or had someone stash it for her. But that's not what I'm looking for when I upend her purse, rummaging among the lipstick and pressed powder and the thin wallet containing only bills and a good, but fake, Norwegian ID, when I kick her legs apart and drag my hands along the expert, expensive seams of her dress. It's information. Something letting me know who she is and why she keeps turning up. I find nothing. I make her take off her shoes anyway—she's still taller than me in her stockinged feet, even though I'm wearing boots—and I run my hands up her legs. Her stockings have seams in the back. They are perfectly aligned with her legs. My hands slip easily up the black material. She's gripping the end of the table now, looking down at me. The look in her eyes does something to me, but I carefully push the feeling away.

"Maybe a little higher," she breathes. I stand up and step back.

"You should know shit could go down here tonight," I say. "So tell me."

She folds her arms. "We could stand here all night and lie to each other. I won't get in your way."

She doesn't. When we move in, she's nowhere to be seen. Whatever she was doing there, she got out quickly.

The third time, I'm bleeding. Another safe house, in South London this time, and we have done something necessary but incredibly illegal. Our country would disavow us if we were caught, and the memory of what I've done is carefully tucked away in the place in my mind where I put these things.

I've been patched up in a different safe house, where they removed the bullet from my shoulder, and where I slept sedated for four hours. Then we had to leave, Derrick and I. We're not even supposed to be in the UK. But here we are.

Another day, another shabby apartment with frayed wallpaper and a kitchen from the 1970s, at best. Derrick dumps me there. He needs to get new papers to get us out of the country and I need to change the bandage on my shoulder. I get some help from a junior British agent—MI5 or MI6, I'm not sure. I'm not sure it matters these days. He has gentle hands. I'm careful not to get any blood on my black fatigues, because I only brought the one pair and I'm not sure when I'll get a chance to change again.

Somewhere in the apartment a phone rings, and he disappears. When he comes back, he's pale.

"Someone's coming in," he says. "I'm supposed to go. I'm sorry."

I'm supposed to wait. I find instant coffee in the fridge and boil water in an electric kettle made of yellowing plastic, and then I sit there, listening to the water come to an excruciatingly slow boil, for several long minutes. A wall clock ticks. The burner phone that's only been in my pocket for a couple of hours beeps with a message. It would be unreadable to anyone but Derrick and me, but the gist is: hang tight, the UK is arranging an airlift. That is unexpected, but then again I've learned that covert operations are never as covert as they are supposed to be.

Then she enters. She's taller than I remember.

"Hello, Emilia," she says. It's her way of letting me know what she knows.

"Florence," I say, showing part of my hand. Two can play that game. "Want some coffee?" She declines. I rummage through the cupboards for a cup and pick a cracked white one with the Royal Air Force logo on the side. I'm not sure Florence is her name—it's the one name she uses the most, as far as I could find after our run-in in Slovenia.

"Well done today," she says, leaning against the fridge. She's cut her hair since then.

"Not sure what you're talking about," I say, stirring water into the instant coffee. The spoon clinks against the edge of the cup. This is why we're lonely, we spooks. It's layer upon layer of lies. I know people who have been married, briefly, pretending like they are traveling three hundred days a year on business. But it wears you down, lying to someone who trusts you with everything. It never lasts.

That is why we're drawn to each other. It's easier with someone who never asks, because they don't want to tell.

I've looked her up by now, and apparently she's looked me up. Her file is sparse, the kind of blankness that lets you know somebody is well above your pay grade. But I've managed to find out some things. She's grown up rich, in one of those families that can trace its roots to before gunpowder reached Europe. I am none of those things, a child of immigrants who died too soon, grown up in rural Texas. She's calm, icy cool. I'm rash and hot. But we have things in common too: she was an officer in the British army for years, reaching the rank of captain before turning covert. I was a Marine before disappearing into black ops. We both have notes from worried psychiatrists in our files. If either of us some day becomes less good at what we do, those notes will come into play. Right now, they need us too much to care.

She stands there, arms folded across her chest, watching me sip my coffee.

"You want something from me," I say. It's not a question.

"What I'm supposed to do here is make sure you leave the country safely. Nobody really wants a loose cannon on the streets right now," she says in that crisp accent that manages to annoy me and turn me on at the same time. I let my gaze glide down her clothes, far less revealing this time: a gray blouse of some soft material, black pants, black shoes. They fit her like they should—draped so that you can just see a hint of round breast, a hint of round hip. She falters for a moment, noticing me looking, but continues: "Your colleague is already en route to a suitable airfield. We figured it was safer to transport you separately. A jet will be ready for you in two hours. We need to leave in a little over one."

That's not really what I meant, and I won't let her get away that easily. "You couldn't task that to the errand boy who was here before?"

"I know what you can do, Emilia. Paris, Ljubljana, Dresden and Beirut last year, Saint Petersburg the year before. Those were all you and your crew, right? I'm not going to leave you with someone green."

"I don't know what you're talking about. So you're the muscle?" I shrug. "Fine by me. What did you want to do for an hour?"

"Let me look at your shoulder." She comes closer. I hold my cup like a shield between us.

"It's okay. I just changed the dressing."

She's close enough that I could grab her and pull her against me. I put my cup down.

"Well, then I just don't know what we should do," she smirks. I grab her.

The door to the bedroom creaks dangerously when we crash into it. Her fingers dig into my neck and her teeth are sunk into my bottom lip. The taste of her kisses is suddenly tinged with iron.

Florence pushes me down on the bed, trying to pull my tank top off, but gives up when faced with the bandage. She pushes it up instead, along with my bra, cool air manifesting as goose bumps on my skin.

She is curiously gentle when touching the shoulder where I've been shot. I want to ask her to prod it, push it, push me—I want pain to rush to my head again, make me dizzy. But then she makes me dizzy, her teeth leaving a trail of smarting skin from the side of my cheek down my chest. She lingers at my breasts, blowing cool air at my nipples, twisting them, biting them. I arch my back, pressing against her, tearing at her clothes.

When she looks up at me, her eyes are dark with need.

I take that moment to relish the reality of this situation. I've dreamed of this ever since I had her pushed against the table in that little room in Ljubljana. Maybe since Paris. She's been on my mind during late nights in cold beds where I've tried and failed to sleep.

I was never a good sleeper.

She tugs at my belt and I reach down to pull her up again. I want to feel her, but she won't let me. "Please," I breathe, and she shakes her head.

"Soon," she says, and the promise makes me tremble.

I never fucking tremble.

But when she has peeled off my pants, she comes up for a kiss. She pushes my good arm above my head, holding it there with more force than is strictly necessary. It's going to leave a bruise, and I'm already looking forward to prodding the sore skin on my transatlantic flight.

"Are you going to be good for me and not move when I let you go?" she asks.

"No," I say. She digs her free hand into my ribs and I yelp at the sudden pressure. "Fine. Maybe."

And then her mouth is gone again.

My body protests, but when I feel her teeth on the inside of my thighs, her nails scratching my hips, it settles.

Her mouth is soft and wet and harsh at the same time, her tongue painting sweet circles around my clit, the reverberations of every move ripping through me like thunder. I want to touch her, but I promised to behave.

My black bush obscures most of her face. Florence moans and her lips vibrate against me while her tongue grows more insistent in smaller, tighter circles and she has me where she wants me, has me bucking against her, has me surrendering, has me coming in her mouth while she licks up every drop of it.

I want a cigarette after, even though it's been years since I stopped. I started because it felt suitable for someone like me. I stopped because I decided I could. The craving is a cliché, like the room around us: impersonal enough to be revealing. But Florence is no cliché, resting her head against my thigh, wiping wetness off her chin.

I cock my head. "Come on," I said. "You promised."

"How are you going to fuck me?" she says, a teasing smile growing on her face. The word sounds all the more enticing when pronounced with that proper accent. "You can barely move your arm."

"I have two arms."

"I would rather have your mouth."

The words rush through me like the swell of another orgasm. I close my eyes. "You can have it," I whisper.

I hear the rustling of her clothes as she undresses, probably folding them neatly beside the bed. Then the bed sinks again, as she makes her way up it. I open my eyes and she's on her knees beside me, gloriously naked. If we had time, we could compare our scars, brag about the people who have tried to kill us and failed. She's got a big one on her thigh. It looks like some kind of shrapnel. I want to reach out and touch it, but that is a level of intimacy beyond what we are doing here. Maybe the fourth time we meet.

"You okay?" she says. I nod. "Let me know if something doesn't work with your injury."

"I like the pain," I say, as if she didn't already know.

"Let's not get blood on the mattress."

She carefully positions her knees on either side of my head, and then the sweet, heady smell of her hits my nose and the taste of her hits my lips and I'm gone. I carefully trace my tongue through her folds, starting with big, slow licks. I savor her. She moves her hips slowly, bracing herself with one hand against the wall.

"Fuck my mouth," I mumble and let my tongue be a little

sharper, a little more precise. She reaches down to thread her
fingers through my hair and holds tight as she thrusts against
me. The sting in my scalp makes my eyes water and I'm licking,
sucking, making a mess. My face is wet and droplets are running
down my neck.

When she comes, she shudders and goes tense, her fist tightening in my hair. I gasp and my mouth fills with her flavor.

Florence is shaking when she climbs off me, leaning against
the wall, chest heaving. I smile up at her.

"How long do we have?" I ask. She leans over to look at her
watch.

"Enough."

"You should get on your back."

"Should I really?" she drawls. "I have you on your back
already, and the view is wonderful."

"Yeah, but I can never come twice. I wanna fuck you though."

"I always did fancy brutish Americans," she smirks, but she
pushes me out of the way and lies down on her side. I pull her
close and kiss her deeply, tasting me on her lips and letting her
taste herself. I push my thigh between her legs and she grinds
against me, digging her nails into my back.

"Brutish but efficient," I say, reaching down to push my
fingers between her slippery folds and my thigh, already wet from
her pushing against it. Two fingers fit easily, but my shoulder is
starting to hurt in an unpleasant way, so I nudge her to get on
her back as I arrange myself between her thighs.

I get better access like this, pushing two fingers inside her,
curling them until I hit the right spot. Her eyes flutter shut and
she moans, louder the harder I fuck her. Her hair is rumpled, her
cheeks are flushed and she's gripping the sheets.

Another finger, and I can feel her stretching around my hand,
accommodating me. She reaches down to touch herself, swiping
at the wetness where I'm pumping in and out of her. She is gentle
with herself, a stark contrast to what we have done to each other,

exploring her hard clit and soft skin. I slow my pace to match hers but she shakes her head.

"Don't stop," she breathes. "Fuck me like you mean it."

I fuck her, and I do mean it. When she comes, she clenches around my hand, her tight, wet pussy contracting and contracting. She grabs my wrist, pushing me deeper inside her, all the while convulsing with closed eyes. Watching her come for me again goes straight to my head like cheap booze. She shudders one last time and then her whole body relaxes. She's still gripping my wrist when she opens her eyes and smiles a sleepy smile at me.

"I wish we could have met under more civilized circumstances this time," she muses.

"The things I could have done to you then," I say. My words make her shudder again, and I pull my fingers out, licking them clean while she watches with parted lips. I settle myself beside her on the bed, both of us on our backs. Not cuddling, but close.

We lie like that for a few minutes, in silence, just breathing. It's a rare moment in my life.

Then it's back to business.

She looks at her watch and clicks her tongue. "Ten minutes," she says. When we are dressed, she sits me down at the kitchen table and checks my bandages, deeming them good enough for now.

"Tell me the plan," I ask, tying my boots. She's eyeing them in a way that I file under things to remember.

"You're flying out of Northolt."

"Who is flying me?"

"Her Majesty's government, on paper. Your people, more likely."

I don't ask if I'll see her again. I don't ask for a number, or even her real name. When the call comes, I take my jacket and my gun and step into the unmarked car pulling to a stop outside the house. The man in the driver's seat doesn't speak during the ride north, and neither do I. I touch the bruise that's already forming on my wrist, my scalp still tingling, my pussy still wet, and the last thing she said before I left rings through my head: "Maybe next time we can spend the night."

A SENSE OF COMING HOME

P. A. Nox

You are here on a whim.

Scratch that, it's a lie. You are here, because you want to be. Because you have craved this moment for the past three years. You took numerous lovers just to forget her, to be rid of her scent on your skin and her taste on your tongue. You are here, because even though you were the one to suggest the amicable split—for everyone's sake, you said—your heart and your body never agreed with your logic.

Put simply, you are here because you have missed her like you'd miss a limb, like you'd miss one of your five senses. Either way, the fact is: you are here.

Here, for the night, means her apartment; it's a new one. She must've moved once she got the job she'd been dreaming of. You haven't seen many of the objects that decorate the place before, but they are undeniably *her*: the practicality, the warmth, the sense that each little thing holds some story, some memory.

There are books on her coffee table that make you smile— history books, of course. If you were to ask her anything, she'd still go into full-on nerd mode and give you stories upon stories of this emperor, or that queen, and so on, until you'd laugh and pull her in for a kiss to shut her up. Your darling know-it-all.

If being the big word here. Because she has been sweet enough to invite you in when you dropped by unannounced, with a bottle of wine to supposedly congratulate her on the promotion. Still, you had to hear about it from a mutual friend. Still, it doesn't mean she will be sweet enough to invite you back into her bed, no matter how quickly you want that to happen. And you do—the instant you step inside, you do.

God, you've missed her. You've missed her laughter and her insanely sharp brain, you've missed her sense of humor and her temper, missed the smell of her skin in the morning, the taste of her at night.

Well, fuck—here you are, already turned on and really pathetic.

You regret ever having let her go. Nobody has measured up to her, and you haven't really allowed anyone to try, because a selfish part of you has always thought this could happen. You'd figure yourselves out, and then you'd meet in the middle again, pick up where you left off. Is this that moment? Or are you just hopeful?

"You look a whole universe away," she says, snapping you out of a contradictory inner rant. She holds out a glass of wine for you to take, and you can't help yourself; you allow your fingers to brush over hers when you grab the stem of the glass, and delectate in the frisson it sends up your spine. (She used to say you like to flirt with danger, so here you are, flirting with the dangerous possibility of rejection.)

You thank her softly, and take a sip, suddenly too wound up to come up with a convincing lie. So you settle for a truth that's easier to say, like: "I'm really proud of you."

The weight of it all settles between you, you think. She looks at you quietly from behind her glass, and you know this is it;

she'll bring up her current girlfriend, or she'll be blunter and tell you right away that you shouldn't even think about it. The two of you are done, and you're the one who came up with the great idea.

"Thanks," she says instead, and you exhale. "The truth is, I don't think I would've found the drive to push myself to get here, if you hadn't—if we had stayed together."

It doesn't hurt, you tell yourself. That's relief, not an ache. "Well, you can tell your people to send me the bill," you try to joke, and it sounds fake but you can't take it back.

"I heard about your successes, too. Youngest R & D director your company's ever had?"

"Eh." You shrug, "You know how it is—it's still pretty much a sausage fest." The two of you share a laugh, and it takes you back a few years, back when you'd keep her up at night with rants about the gap between men and women in STEM. But you're not here to talk shop. It's fake, this whole patting each other on the back ever so politely, thinking it's possible to avoid the elephant in the room.

"I'm glad you came," she says, and it floors you.

"You're—I thought you'd be mad."

She shrugs lightly. "I was, for the first year. But it pushed me to get myself together, and I'd be lying to myself if I pretended like I'm not grateful to you. You were the little voice in my ear."

You'd give a lot to be the little voice in her ear again. Fuck. "I missed you."

The silence settles between you again. You went and screwed up, you think. You had no right, no right to come back and—

"I missed you, too," she admits on an exhale. The knot in your throat disappears. You grin; she smiles back at you.

"Is there anyone—"

"No. Single. You?"

"No." You set the wineglass down, and shift closer. "Could I—can I—"

She lets out a breathless laugh and reaches out to grab the front of your button-up shirt, and says "God, come here."

She still laughs when she kisses. She still tastes better than wine, better than honey, better than anything you've ever put your mouth on. Her fingers curl and press over the back of your neck, and draw you closer, so you kiss her on shaky grounds until your heart settles. Then, you show her how much you've missed her.

Her lips part easily when you lick at the seam of them, her tongue coming out to meet yours before you can even hope for it. She isn't smiling anymore, but neither are you. "Missed—" you try to say. "Yeah," she tells you right back. Her fingers are at the buttons of your shirt now, two already open by the time you reach down and stall her with a gentle grip.

"I wanna do this in a bed," you confess. You've dreamed of it, after all; her body naked and sprawled on the bed, your head between her legs, her arching back and her quivering thighs. Holy hell, have you ever dreamed of it.

She takes one look at you, probably reading you down to your soul, and pulls you up from the couch. Three years is a very long time, and you don't doubt that she found some way to move on from you just like you attempted to do the same. Right now, however, as you follow her down the hallway feeling happier and fuller than in the past three years, you realize you were an idiot to think that you weren't even worthy of attempting the whole long-distance thing first. Maybe you could've survived it; you two could've survived anything, just look at you now.

But then again, maybe not. Maybe you would have given in to frustration after a couple of months and a whole continent apart, and tossed aside literally everything for the sake of a grand, reckless gesture. You did the right thing, you did, you did. You tell yourself this over and over, unaware that you've slowed down and she's looking at you with concern.

You answer her questioning gaze with a blunt, "I shouldn't

have let you go." It aches to let the words out, but it aches more to want everything back to the way it was, when both of you have changed. All you can wish for is the chance to rediscover.

She steps closer to you and pulls you in for a hug in the middle of her hallway, making you feel both very small and vulnerable in her arms, and at the same time insanely safe. "So don't let me go now," she murmurs against your shoulder, and you realize that the elephant in the room isn't that you still want her. It's that you still love her.

"Never again," you promise, "if you'll let me." She gives you the answer in the shape of a kiss, taking the lead on this one and stealing your breath with the ferocity of it. You respond in turn, revived and stoked after that whole exchange, more at ease.

Now you have this feeling like you are allowed to tease, so you bite her lower lip and run your nails down her back over her clothes, ready to swallow her gasp with another kiss. There it is, and there you go, kissing her again until your lips hurt, swaying on your feet and pulling her along with you in this feverish dance.

A few more steps, and because you have no idea which door leads to her bedroom, you press her against the wall, and set your mouth on the side of her neck. She gasps and you let out a soft chuckle, because your sweet girl still has her weak spots. You know this body like it's a map you drew yourself. You know how to gradually make your way to her breasts, how to make her gasp by the time you get there.

Sweet little kisses down the side of her neck, your fingers pulling the collar of her shirt aside to suck on the skin above her collarbone. Her hands are getting more and more frantic on your back, and it gives you life. You blow cold air over the skin you just kissed, and watch as goose bumps bloom down from her neck to the top of her breasts. You're getting there.

You pull back to look up at her, her lips swollen from kissing, her face flushed and her eyes dark with want, and it's a face you're so familiar with it hurts in the best of ways. You tug her shirt out of her skirt and push your hand up under it, feeling the softness of her skin, the heat that emanates from it; she's still a furnace when she's horny, and you want to make that joke again about how you got her all hot and bothered, but she's digging her nails into your shoulders. So that's a cue to pull her shirt up to reveal her breasts, and kiss them hello, on top of her bra.

"Missed you," you murmur against the fabric of her bra, finding a pebbled nipple and licking at it until it she shivers.

"Me or the boobs?" she manages to ask, and you laugh, bite her gently, and watch her jump.

"You? The breasts? Maybe both?" Before she can protest, you sink to your knees. "But hello, you in a skirt?" She is grinning down at you, looking unintentionally coy, as if she doesn't know where you're going. You run your hands up the back of her calves, the back of her thighs, her ass. You've missed every inch of her, and you're going to kiss every inch of her, too, but not right now. Right now, it's a rush to remember all the really good spots, which is why you pull her underwear down to her ankles, and put your head up under her skirt. She steps out of her underwear and stands with her legs slightly apart, and in the dim light beneath her skirt you can trace the outline of her cunt. Not that sight matters, since it's taste that you're going for.

A quick taste at first, tongue slipping over her folds very lightly; she's wet, deliciously slick on your tongue, so you probe deeper. Spread her pussy lips with the next lick, suckle at her clit, all nice and wet. Holy shit, you've missed this, you've missed her, and sex with her, and eating her out.

There's suddenly light, and you glance up from where you're at, your mouth fastened to her clit, your tongue drawing gentle circles, and find her watching you. She's pulled her skirt up, and lost her shirt when you weren't looking, as well as her bra. She looks gorgeous, one hand holding the skirt out of the way so she can watch you eating her out, and the other teasing at her breasts. You both share a silent grin, just before she pinches one of her nipples and you close your eyes and go back to it.

You move by whim and sound. Lick into her, lap at her clit, suck at her labia, and listen. Soak up every gasp, every breathless rendition of your name. You hum when she slips and calls you *baby* again, oh so pleading. She wants fingers, you know that's what it means, but she's not getting them yet. This moment right here is because you were so grateful and so impatient, but she'll still have to wait for the bedroom for the real fuck. You're going to take her for hours. When she squirms in protest, you don't think twice before reaching around and swatting her ass very lightly, one, two. That makes her gush against your tongue, and grind against your mouth when you push your tongue inside her.

You're out of breath, so you kiss the tops of her thighs to prevent yourself passing out from overexcitement, but you never think to wipe your mouth clean of her arousal. Two seconds is all you need, before going back between her legs. *Come on, babe, I have all day,* you want to tell her. Your knees hurt, but you're going to stay here until she shakes with a well-deserved orgasm.

You duck again to kiss her opening, to pierce her with your tongue, and let out a thrilled moan when she brings her hand down from her breast to rub her clit without a second thought. She twitches against your tongue, fluttery and hot, and you know she's close by the way she's squeezed her eyes shut and keeps forgetting to breathe.

This is it; you remember every trick in the book, everything that worked for her before. Squeeze her ass and hold her still while you fuck her, hum when she tries to ride your mouth and almost stumbles, and when her breath hitches, oh so telling, you pull your hand away and suck at the spot above her clit until she comes. It's the most beautiful thing you've seen in a while, and you look at pictures of space on a daily basis.

You lick her through it until she stops shaking and pushes you lightly away as a sign to stop, and finally you remember to breathe. Deep inhale, shaky exhale, followed by a laugh. Your knees are chaffed, your inner thighs feel wet, and her come is ticklish on your chin, but you've never been happier.

"Come here," she begs, and bends over to kiss you. You're both this close to ending up kneeling on the floor in her hallway and just fucking each other silly right then and there, and while on any other night this will be a perfectly acceptable option, tonight it's just been a detour. So with some reluctance and a sigh into her mouth, you pull yourself together and stand up again. She pulls you into a hug first, and another kiss, before taking you into the bedroom; what do you know, you'd knelt between her legs just next to the bedroom door.

It's not a big room, not that you get to take much of it in; she doesn't so much show you in as tug you inside and throw you on her bed.

"Listen, you're not the only one who's missed this," she tells you in lieu of explanation, and gets you naked. Her hands pull both your jeans and underwear down in one go, together with your shoes. She's still very efficient, and you're still incredibly turned on by this part, by how quickly she'll get you naked.

You shift backward until your head's on her pillows, and she climbs in bed with you after taking her skirt off and being left naked, at last. You still have your shirt and bra on, but apparently she's decided that fair is fair and you get to take those off yourself if you want them off. What you really want, though, is her mouth on you, so you spread your legs.

"Look at you," she murmurs, and she touches you. She spreads your folds with two clever fingers, and reaches up to give you a taste of yourself. You suck on her fingers without breaking eye contact, turned on beyond the ability to tease. She pulls her fingers out and leans over you, naked and gorgeous and all yours again. "What?" she asks you, soft and teasing.

"What do you want? Hmm?" Her hand moves back between your legs, and she fills you—fuck, she fills you up, two fingers in two slick thrusts, and you nearly come just like that. "Is this what you want?"

"Yes," you manage to get out, shaky and breathless, grabbing for her as best you can; you touch her cheek, her hair, her breast, her hip. She's hyper-focused now, because she doesn't even shiver when you grab her ass, she just curls her fingers inside you slowly and with deadly precision, and you shake. You also curse, something filthy and foul, soft, but not inaudible. It makes her laugh (you want that, you do), but it also makes her pull her fingers out and then push them in with a slap of flesh against flesh. You curse again.

"Come again?" she teases.

"I'm *trying*," you grit out, and laugh because it's easier than begging and easier than riding her fingers right now. Mostly because she pulls them out of you again and sucks them clean, and all you're left with is laughter and watching her like she's a sunrise.

She leans over you and kisses you very softly, and you shiver under her. "Shh, baby, I've got you now." Then she moves, your generous tease, not a devil in disguise but the most perfect woman you've ever met. She moves between your legs, and hooks your right knee over her shoulder and licks you open.

You arch from that first lick, and grab at her bedsheets while she kisses you again, openmouthed and purposefully dirty, because she remembers you like it like that; you love hearing how wet you are when she eats you out. She sucks, she kisses and licks, she teases and then nips, she makes you climb and climb until you're on the crest of it, at the very edge. Then, "Want it?"

"Yes!" you scream, you beg, you grab for her hair and move her closer, and she gets you coming with nothing more than a few soft licks.

You'd resent how easy that was, if not for having missed it so.

Besides, by the time you finally come down from the first climax, you're too pleased and full to resent anything. Not even the fact that she keeps licking you.

"Can you still go all night?" she asks between kisses, not moving from between your legs. You glance down at her, feeling wrung out for now, and let out a little laugh. She's rocking her hips against the mattress.

"Can you?" you ask her right back.

As an answer, she sucks on your slick pussy lips until you let your head drop back again, and let go. She pulls you over the edge one more time in a matter of seconds, not that you were counting. This time, you come with her name on your lips instead of a breathless gasp, and it's satisfying down to the marrow of your bones.

Honestly, you know she could stay there for hours until you were worn out from it, but you want her more than just like this tonight, so you eventually pull her up. As soon as you kiss her again, as soon as she presses her naked body against yours, you forget about every potential plan and just settle into relishing it. The touch, the warmth, the taste and feel of her; it makes you feel just a little complete, and you're too drunk in love right now to be scared of it.

It leaves you both a little breathless, because she breaks the kiss eventually to rest on top of you, and you go on for minutes just holding each other in silence. There will be time to talk, later. There will be time to plan, time to figure out how to never lose this again.

For now, you only want to get to know her again.

You roll her gently on her back and kiss her lips very lightly, before pulling yourself together and getting up. "I'll go get the wine," you let her know, and go back to the living room for the glasses and the bottle. When you get back into the bedroom, you find her sprawled in bed under the covers, looking satisfied and happy, and you're filled with a feeling of belonging. Of coming back home.

She pulls the covers back and pats the spot next to her, and you join her, just like that. There will be a time for losing the rest of your clothes later, too. For now, you're going to bask.

It's the best choice you've made in a while.

ABOUT THE AUTHORS

VALERIE ALEXANDER lives in Los Angeles. Her work has been previously published in *Best of Best Women's Erotica*, *The Big Book of Domination*, *Best Lesbian Erotica* and other anthologies.

EVEY BRETT (eveybrett.wordpress.com) lives in the Arizona desert with two cats and a Lipizzan mare and enjoys hiking national parks to discover bits of local history to use in her stories. She's also been published in *Best Gay Erotica of the Year* and *Best Women's Erotica 2015*.

GEONN CANNON is the author of over thirty novels, including *Gemini* and the Golden Crown Literary Society Best Novel Award winner, *Dogs of War*, as well as *Trafalgar & Boone*, which was named to *Kirkus Reviews'* Best Books of 2015. Geonn lives in Oklahoma.

VANESSA DE SADE is a forty-something full-figure gal who writes about real women exploring the darker regions of sexuality. She is the author of two novels and the solo story collections *Fur, Black & White Movies, Nude Shots, In the Forests of the Night* and *Tales from a Tangled Bush*.

TAYLOR C. DUNNE is a New York–based writer and artistic dilettante who plays well with both cats and dogs.

UK based **CAMILLE DUVALL**'s career in drama development inspired her to work on projects that challenge the lack of credible lesbian characters in film and on TV. Initially writing short stories as gifts for her partner, Camille has been encouraged to widen her audience.

V. FLORIAN is a Swedish writer who has published three novellas, including *När temperaturen stiger*, in the *Queerlequin* series by publisher Genusredaktörerna, and enjoys the borders that can be crossed in anonymity.

With stories in more than forty anthologies, **TAMSIN FLOWERS** (tamsinflowers.com) has probably been writing erotica for far too long, but she isn't going to stop. Having completed her year-long *Alchemy xii* BDSM novella series, she's now turning her attention to a new novel of a dark and twisty hue.

SACCHI GREEN (sacchi-green.blogspot.com) has published stories in a hip-high stack of erotica anthologies, including *She Who Must Be Obeyed* and eight volumes of *Best Lesbian Erotica*, and edited a dozen anthologies, among them *Best Lesbian Erotica 20th Anniversary Edition* and Lambda Award winners *Lesbian Cowboys* and *Wild Girls, Wild Nights*.

ELNA HOLST writes lesbian erotica and romance, reads Tolstoy and plays contract bridge. Her effusions have appeared in *The New Urge Reader 2* (Black Scat Books), *Pure Lust* (Black Scat Review #14) and *From Top to Bottom* (Ladylit Publishing).

DEB JANNERSON (deborahjannerson.com) is a New Orleans–based poet and novelist. Her book of poetry, *Rabbit Rabbit*, was published by Finishing Line Press in 2016. Her work has appeared in *Best Lesbian Erotica 2015*, *My Gay New Orleans* and over a dozen magazines.

ROXY KATT is a Canadian who writes lesbian and phallogyne erotica (a term she prefers to "futa" or "shemale") and specializes in stories of comical humiliation. The dominant fetish elements in her work include leather, rubber and armor.

J. BELLE LAMB holds an MFA in poetry. She lives on an island in the Pacific Northwest. Her story "Serious Swimmer" recently appeared in the anthology *From Top to Bottom: Lesbian Stories of Dominance and Submission*. She's active in her local kink scene and always easily distracted by hot women.

ANNABETH LEONG (Twitter @AnnabethLeong) is frequently confused about her sexuality but enjoys searching for answers. She is the author of the butch-femme BDSM novella *Heated Leather Lover*, and the editor of *Maker Sex: Erotic Stories of Geeks, Hackers, and DIY Projects*.

SAMANTHA LUCE lives in the Mosquito state, aka Florida. She works in law enforcement. In her spare time, she writes fan fiction, reads whatever she can get her hands on and is currently at work on a lesbian thriller featuring a kick-ass FDLE agent and a sexy deputy sheriff.

MEGAN MCFERREN (Twitter @inarcadiamegan) is a New York–based writer who loves pushing boundaries and exploring queer relationships, especially those set long ago and far away. She spends her days working in Internet security and her nights writing torrid stories.

P. A. NOX finds an active imagination and some spare time make for a lot more erotica short stories than anyone would eagerly admit to having written during brunch with friends. But everyone has their secrets, and some are meant to be shared. This is just the beginning.

RADCLYFFE is the author of over fifty lesbian romances and dozens of short stories and has edited numerous anthologies. She is a multi-Lambda Literary Award winner and recipient of the 2014 Dr. James Duggins Outstanding Mid-Career Novelist Prize from the Lambda Literary Foundation.

ABOUT THE EDITOR

D. L. KING (dlkingerotica.blogspot.com) has a tiny, postage stamp-sized garden where she likes to entertain friends with tasty barbecue and all manner of libation. She lives with a literary-minded cat who begs for treats from about 8:00 P.M. on, except when her mistress is working at the computer. While other cats like to sit on keyboards and sleaze their way in front of your monitor, Bat Girl knows how important the work of writing and editing is and refuses to bother her during those times. (No, really, it's true.) She must be a very patient cat as D. L. is almost always at the computer. D. L. King is the editor of thirteen anthologies, including a Lambda Literary Award winner, *The Harder She Comes: Butch/Femme Erotica*, a Lambda Literary Award finalist, *Where the Girls Are: Urban Lesbian Erotica* and four Independent Publisher medalists, *Carnal Machines: Steampunk Erotica*; *The Harder She Comes: Butch/Femme Erotica*; *Under Her Thumb: Erotic Stories of Female Domination* and *The Big Book of Domination: Erotic Fantasies*. Her short stories have been published in close to a hundred anthologies, including six volumes of *Best Lesbian Erotica*, as well as titles such as *Say Please: Lesbian BDSM Erotica*; *Girl Crazy: Coming Out Erotica*; *Girl Fever: 69 Stories of Sudden Sex for Lesbians*; *Girls Who Score: Hot Lesbian Erotica* and *Appetites: Tales of Lesbian Lust*. D. L. King is also the editor of *She Who Must Be Obeyed: Femme Dominant Lesbian Erotica*; *Slave Girls: Erotic Stories of Submission*; *Seductress: Erotic Tales of Immortal Desire*; *The Sweetest Kiss: Ravishing Vampire Erotica*; *Spankalicious: Adventures in Spanking*; *Spank* and *Voyeur Eyes Only*. She is the author of the novellas *Stubborn as a Bull*, *A Scarlet Christmas*, and *The Marrying Kind*, a collection of short stories, *Her Wish is Your Command: 21 Erotic Fem Dom Stories* and two novels, *The Melinoe Project* and *The Art of Melinoe*.